Any Girl Who Loves The Beatles Is Bound To Break Your Heart

Nick Pollack

Based on the original screenplay 'Any Girl Who Loves
The Beatles Is Bound To Break Your Heart'.

Written by Nick Pollack & Ryan Hayward

ISBN: 9781521348932
ISBN-13: 9781521348932

For no one.

CHAPTER ONE

YESTERDAY

My dad's your quintessential man of few words.

It's not that he hates talking, or people for that matter, but his comfort level in any situation is directly proportional to the number of words he speaks.

So, when he does let his guard down to pass on some insight, I'd tend to listen.

The pieces of wisdom he'd acquired over the years on women for instance — the ones he felt paternally compelled to impart — boiled down to two points:

One: "All women, at least the ones worth knowing, are crazy. Rationalise it however you want, Grant", he'd pontificate, "but happiness is finding the least crazy one & making her yours."

The other: "Any girl who loves the Beatles is bound to break your heart."

Now, the first one makes sense, in my experience anyway — even if meant as a throwaway line from a father unaccustomed to outward signs of affection, fumbling to find the right words to console a son's freshly broken heart — there's still an element of bittersweet truth to it.

At the same time, whenever he dropped that nugget of wisdom, mum would always chime in with "You're right, all women are crazy. But only because all men are stupid."

So, while the first point could just as easily have been relayed from a mother to a daughter about what dopes us guys are, it was the second one — passed on when I was only twelve — which always struck a deeper chord.

Why he told me, I can't even remember, but its effect was to make me seek out *everything* that there was to know about this band that would predestine women to break hearts (admittedly, the already categorically insane if we're going to deal in mildly offensive mass generalisations of course).

Over the years though, I've drawn my own conclusions about the theory. And I think it boils down to this.

You can *like* the Beatles; you can enjoy listening to them. You can know all the words to a song without even knowing its name — or that it's even one of their songs.

But to *love* the Beatles — to truly get them — is to see life in a totally different way... and it makes you question how their music, something so apparently simple, can have such a significant effect on you.

Why can't everything in life be as simple as a Beatles song?

…why can't love?

Why is this of any significance? Well, for the simple fact that if mum hadn't been a Stones fan, this story would never have taken place.

CHAPTER TWO

SIX AM

Ticket money passport. Ticket money passport.

Hmmm...two outta three will have to do.

Shit, did I check my passport is still valid?!

...expires March 18, 2019.

Phew, I'm good.

OK, one last final check of the bathroom.

All clear there.

Under the bed.

A bit of dust. Landlord can sort that. Better grab those Smirnoff bottles though.

Ummmm... top of the kitchen cupboard.

Ahh-ha, so that's where my copy of "Rubber Soul" went. Guess I'll leave it as a house warming present for the new tenants.

This apartment's as clean as it's gonna get under my watch.

The times I've had in here; the best of... the worst of.

Wonder if they'll take those holes in the ceiling out of my deposit? Wish I could remember how they got there?

Time check — 6.06

I was really hoping that nap would help me find the words, but I'm still drawing a blank.

Sit down and start with a fresh page. Now let's see...

How about "Darling Abi..."

ERRRR God no.

Scrunch that one up. Aim for the bin...

It's game seven of the NBA championship.

The Clipper's season all comes down to this bucket.

Two point five seconds on the clock...

CP3's on the arc...

He shoots!

He... almost scores.

OK, new page, let's try again.

Hmmmm... come on Grant Alan Ryder! Prove that those four years you dedicated to perfecting your air hockey game, general public affray and intense procastibation all in the pursuit of that shiny, useless arts degree weren't wasted. What have you got in you?!

"Abi, what a difference a year makes huh..."

Urghhhhh. Bor-RING!

Come on brain, work!

For once, tell her how you feel. Find the words to win her back. To get her to stop you from leaving.

If only words could change everything.

Actually, that's not bad, "...if only words could change everything."

Right, well that's the first line done.

What's next...?

A romantic sonnet?

A declaration of undying love?

A dirty limerick?

What about "Til there was you in my life, every little thing was..............."

GGGAAAAAHHHHHHHH!!!

This is terrible.

Maybe I should have a drink, it always makes me more lucid.

NO.

NO.

NO NO NO NO NO!

This is day one of your new life.

No more drinking.

No more drugs.

No more living in the past.

No more —

—BANG BANG BANG—

'OK SID I'LL BE DOWN IN A MINUTE! Stop bangin' on the roof!'

That old coot's rambunctious this morning.

OK, so we have: "Abi, what a difference a year makes huh? If only words could change everything... PS, I love you."

Hardly a Shakespearean soliloquy but it'll have to do for now,

I'll finish it on the ride to the airport—

—BANG BANG BANG BANG —

Calm down you mad buggar, I'm coming.

Right, well "place I've called home for the last five years", this is it. Thanks for the memories, the good and the bad. Don't forget to write and all that.

OK, keys left on the side table, garbage you're

coming with me.

Two very rugged duffel bags held together with gaffer tape and high hopes — check.

Old brown shoes, unfortunately, you're coming on this journey too.

Thanks everyone, you've been a wonderful audience, you really have. Tonight's my last show, and you've been great, really the best audience a little ol' me could have wanted, try the veal and don't forget to tip your waitress—

— BANGBANGBANGBANGBANGBANG— GRRRRRR. I'M COMING!

And… lights out.

'Ladies and Gentlemen, this is your captain again. We'll be starting our descent into Sydney's Kingsford Smith Airport very soon. If you'd please fasten your seat belts and secure your tray tables...'

Where's that bloody phone?

What corner of my bag are you hiding?

Seriously, who needs all this crap in their bag?!

That's it, as soon as I get to the hotel, I'm doing a purge — everything that I do not immediately require is gone.

May as well add Pete to the purge as well.

Lying fuckwit.

Grrrr, don't think about it.

This seat is so uncomfortable. What is this airline? Must remember to make sure they never book me on it again.

Food was meh ok.

I'm completely knackered, got no sleep. Those

sleeping tablets were absolute duds. Last time I take pharmaceutical advice from a Japanese A&R manager.

'Miss Taylor, would you please bring your seat in the upright position.'

'I'm sorry, of course.'

Why do we as a nation apologise for things like that? The English way, 'oh I'm terribly sorry' at the drop of a hat. Besides, I'm not actually sorry, I was bloody comfortable! Well, comparatively.

Not gonna argue with her though. That poor flight attendant looks more exhausted than I do. I don't know how they do it, stuck in a plane dealing with wallies twenty-four seven. Worse than being in the music industry.

Right, back to work... OK, now Instagram Instagram where can you be — hmmm, when did I move its app? Weird.

Anyway, and… record.

Wait, is it recording?

It is.

'Hey guys, guess where I'm heading today, lemme just turn this to the window and maybe you can see that big white curvy building on the harbour, and the bridge that looks kinda like a coat hanger. Yep, see you soon Sydney. First time, can't wait. EKK!'

And save.

Hopefully that'll satiate the PR guys for today. I can't be bollocksed doing social media updates, today of all days.

God, Pete's a such a dickhead. Why couldn't he have just done it behind my back and confessed all when I returned. Now he's told me the night before this show and completely ballsed up my headspace.

Well if it looks like a dog, and smells like a dog, it's probably Pete.

Adios.

OK, breathe in, breathe out, breathe in....

Gotta admit, it's a pretty spectacular view though.

OK Sydney, talk to me, what have you got in store for me today, huh?

'You took your bleedin' time getting downstairs.'

'Sid, I had to pack up my apartment.'

'Hide all the dead hookers you mean.'

'If you're going to be mean Mr Mustard, I may as well be on my way now. Stop giving me grief.'

'Don't get your knickers in a knot sweetheart. Grab a seat.'

'Why don't you get some light in here? I don't know how many times I've told you to open these curtains. There we go — ahhh, good day sunshine! Isn't that better?'

'I ain't planning on photosynthesising — close 'em!'

'The government's got better things to do than spy on an eighty year old man—'

'—CLOSE EM! And everybody's got something to hide.'

'Suit yourself. You're really in a mood this morning, aren't you? What are you looking for over there anyway?'

'Just be patient, I'll show ya in a minute.'

'You could have at least put some pants on.'

'Nothing you ain't seen before.'

'Sadly.'

'Just sit down and don't bother me. I poured you a whiskey, That one just there on the ledge.'

'No thanks.'

'Whaddaya mean no!'

'I told you two days ago, I'm going clean from today.'

'You, going clean? Ha! I give you twenty-four hours.'

'Thanks for the moral support.'

'Pleasure. Shove over so I can sit too.'

'Sit on your own chair.'

'Fine. Here, I've kept this for you for when the right day arrived.'

'A dirty, coffee-stained envelope?'

'Sherlock's got nothing on you kid. No, don't open it now.'

'Ugh, close your legs!'

'It's my house. Shhesh.'

'Look, thank you, I really appreciate the gesture, but I can't take your money.'

'HA! You think I can live in this bastard of a city and afford to give my money away. Just open it when you've left. It'll come in handy. Pop it in your bag for later.'

'What are you looking for now?'

'A lighter. Can never find the damn things when you need one.'

'What are you doing smoking? Gimme it!'

'HEY! Why'd you do that?!'

'You've been told not to!'

'You didn't need to break it. You rat.'

'NO SMOKING! We're serious.'

'Taking away any pleasure left a dying old man.'

'You're not dying.'

'I am.'

'You will be soon if you don't behave.'

'Hmph. So, did you tell your old man yet that you're leaving?'

'Hasn't cared what I've been doing the last year, can't see why what I'm doing today makes a difference.'

'Things'll change kid. Always do. That reminds me — d'you ever hear the tale of the two frogs. Japo frogs I think. One leaves, I'll say, Kyoto, other leaves Osaka or some such and they cross paths on the top of a mountain. Kyoto frog says, 'is that town better than mine?', the other says, 'I don't know, I can't see yours from here.' So they stand on each other's shoulders and look at the towns and realise there's not that much difference between the two... oh... damn.'

'What?'

'I just forgot the point of that bleedin' story.'

'I think I get it.'

'Make more sense if they were French. They're frogs, right?'

'I'll miss the casual racism you'll bring to my life, Sid.'

'Well, I won't miss having my light fittings rattle as you root those hippos you kept bringing home.'

'I don't have the energy to trade barbs with you this morning old man.'

'Lightweight.'

'Anyway, back to that matter at hand. So, Michelle, the lady from over the road —'

'—The 'spic with the big cans?'

'Be nice. And don't say that. She's a lovely lady. She'll check in on you, so long as you don't offend her.'

'Yeah yeah. What happened to the other one? Sexy Sadie, grrrrr!'

'She's leaving home and going to study in Bathurst so she can't come around anymore.'

'Shame. So... you're really not going to have a drink with me?'

'I'm sorry Sid, but... I just want to start clean.'

'Sure kid. I get it. Quite a thing ain't it?'

'What is?'

'Knowing it's the last time you'll ever see someone. Never gets easier.'

'I'll miss you Sid. Thank you for being a friend to me these last few years.'

'Likewise kid. Likewise. Well, if you ain't gonna share a drink with me, least you can do is play a few rounds of poker.'

'A few games for old times' sake. That I can do. Where are the cards? Still in the desk drawer?'

'No, this calls for the special cards.'

'Not your nudie girls from the 70's cards?'

'Yes, these very ones which I had ready and waiting. Your deal.'

Time check — 6.16.

'OK, hand 'em here. A quick shuffle and.... Ewwww!!'

'What?'

'These two cards are stuck together!'

'Oh, calm down... Ahhh, the five of spades. To be forty years younger.'

'You're really gross.'

'Shut up and deal!'

'Catch ya round kid.'

'Not if I don't see you first old man. See ya Sid.'

Wow. That was tough.

I'm really never going to see that guy ever again.

I'm gonna miss him.

Oh shit, Dave's on his phone at the end of the hall... think I might sneak out the other way. Do not want to run into him today...

'Yeah, yeah, oh hang on a sec, I might have another option — HEY GRANT, WAIT UP!'

Damn.

'Hey Dave. What's up?'

'Ryder, I need a favour.'

'Well surely it's not fashion advice cause you're rocking that fluffy pink dressing gown. Do they make them for men?'

'What? Oh, this? It's Rita's. Look I need you to do a job for me. Two people have called in sick... even though I saw them both at the Spiegeltent last night until closing, bum drunks. Anyway, I'd love you to fill in and chaperone around one of the overseas acts I'm looking after.'

'Really? After what I did the last time?'

'Believe me, that's exactly how desperate I am. Look all you gotta do is take 'em for a little sightseeing — there's the bridge, there's a cockatoo — then get em to soundcheck. I'll pay you double.'

'Can't.'

'Triple!'

And right on cue, the gaffer tape holding my bag

together decides to give way.

Perfect.

'Great. Look I'd help if I could — I can obviously use the coin — but I fly out in four hours.'

'Oh yeah, the big trip. Oh well, worth a shot.'

'No worries, I hope you can sort something out.'

'Cheers. Oh and... look after yourself, OK?'

'I will. And say goodbye to the lovely Rita for me.'

Well that wasn't as awkward as I thought it might be. Time heals all wounds I guess.

'Passport please — holiday or business?'

'Work, I'm performing at the Sydney Festival tonight, here's all my paperwork.'

Here it comes........

...and

...bingo.

There it is, the 'should I know who you are' look.

'Nina Taylor huh? Are you as famous as that lady Madonna?'

'Haha, no not quite, unfortunately.'

'Oh. Should I know your stuff?'

'Maybe, do you listen to much radio?'

'Only talkback.'

'Well perhaps not then.'

'OK, how long you here for?

'One night in Sydney. Melbourne tomorrow. Then back to Europe in two days.'

Come on come on Mr Passport Control man,

just do the stamp thing.

Grrrr, why do they always draw this out?! Every single time.

'OK, enjoy your stay.'

'Thanks.'

'And have a great show.'

'Oh, you too.'

You too?!

I'm such a pillock.

I need a coffee.

'And it's coming up to 6.37 this morning on what promises to be a scorcher of a Saturday here in Sydney. Whatever you do today folks make sure you keep well hydrated. I know that the city will be heaving tonight with the first weekend of events for the Sydney Festival, so that's going to cause a lot of...'

'Can you turn the radio down please?'

'Pardon?'

'CAN YOU TURN THE RADIO DOWN?'

I have to get the one deaf Uber driver in Sydney.

'Better?'

'Thanks. So, it's just up ahead.'

'You aren't going to the airport?'

'Later, I'm seeing my sister first.'

'Ah, I was wondering why you wanted me to take you in the wrong direction.'

And Sydney's nosiest Uber driver.

'WHOA! There must be like a million comics in here, uncle Grant!'

'A few hundred, maybe.'

I love kids. So easy to please.

'Wow, The Death of Superman! These are great! Thank you.'

'You're welcome, but remember these are very special to me, some I've had since I was your age, so I want you to promise to look after them really well until I get back OK, big guy?'

'Uh-uh, I promise. So, uncle Grant, when will you be back?'

The innocent questions of kids.

I can't tell him the truth, so I'll just change the subject.

'I like your bird. When did you get her?'

'Him.'

'When did you get him?'

'Three months ago.'

'I guess it's been a while since I visited. What's his name?'

'Rocky Racoon.'

'Hmmm... interesting name for a bird, and can your bird sing?'

'Not really, only a northern song, a bit of it.'

And on cue, here's the sister from the black swamp.

'I do have actual things to do today.'

'OK, we're coming.'

'I'll be in the car.'

I swear her hoofs get louder each time I see her.

'She always this cranky, kiddo?'

'Just the last few weeks.'

So right around the time I told her I was leaving then.

'Alright, come on champ, best get a move on before the dragon lady bites our heads off. Bring a couple of those to read in the car if you want.'

CHAPTER THREE

SEVEN AM

Right Grant, focus now and get back to this masterpiece of literature...

"Abigail, what a difference a year makes..."

My god, it's just so monumentally crap.

Scrunch that up, wind down the window and — see ya.

'Did you just throw something out of the car?'

'Watch the road!'

'Did you?'

'Yeah. So?'

'DON'T! I don't want the kid thinking it's OK.'

'Calm down sis.'

'Don't tell me to calm down. And stop fighting with the air conditioner.'

'But it's boiling.'

'Yeah mum, it's boiling.'

'See.'

'Oh darling just read your comic please.'

Well, this is the car ride from hell. Perhaps the radio can fill this painfully awkward silence.

'—listeners there's road closures at the lower end of the city tonight for the festival so make sure you take that into account with—'

'And don't play with my radio!'

'What crawled up you and died?'

'Did something crawl into mum?'

'No Matt, uncle Grant is being extremely rude.'

'You're swerving all over the road.'

'Today Grant? Today of all days you decide to leave?'

'Give it a rest Emily. You know why I need to do this. You know it ain't easy... you know how hard it can be.'

'Your solution for everything right. Just run away from it. Like father like son.'

Ahh, to have a beer right now so I could hold it aloft and say I'd drink to that....

Probably wouldn't go down too well. That reminds me...

'Em, can you spot me a hundred?'

'Unbelievable!'

'My last pay check goes through this week, but I'm a bit skint til then. I'll pay you right back.'

'HA! You already owe me over two grand. No chance.'

Tight arse.

Are we there yet?

There's one guitar...

...come on, where's the other one.

Pleeeeeeeeeeease don't tell me they've lost it.

The crowd's all thinned out now and I'm the loser standing here by the baggage carousel waiting for it to go around and around, all the while my Fender gently weeps on its way for a two-week vacay in god knows where.

Great.

Welcome to Sydney indeed. Can this day just be over already?!

Was that my phone? I think so.

I seriously need to purge all this crap in my bag. Do I really need to keep the instructions for that travel hairdrier anymore? Especially after it broke on the first use. Ah, there you are phone.

Ugh, another text from the lovely Pete.

'I'm so sorry'

And by a process of elimination... Peter Mazin, you and your "sorry" are hereby blocked from my phone.

Ahh, that was quite satisfying actually. I should have done that years ago.

So let's see — they serve lousy food, had crudy chairs and now they've probably lost my guitar. Well, I sure won't be flying them again.

Where's the lost baggage counter in this place... better ask that security gent.

'Sorry sir—'

There's that damned redundant 'sorry' again Nina, you ninny.

'—pardon me, but where's the lost baggage counter?'

'Just over in that corner Miss.'

'Right, thank you.'

OK bags, come on, off we go.

I did not need *this* this morning.
Of all mornings.
I need that coffee.

'What airline are you flying?'
'Virgin Atlantic — just pull in up here.
Whoaaaaaa, easy on the brakes there sis.'
'Are we getting out mum?'
'Just stay in the car Matt.'
'Can you pop the boot? Thanks.'
I'm glad *that* ride's over. Jeez. Anyway… OK,
so got my two bags, and one backpack and close
the boot — BANG — and now I'll just walk
around to her door to say goodb—
—Oh.
Wow.
Did she really just do that?!
Did she really just speed off?!
Without saying goodbye. Really?
Wow.
I… she…
…Wow.
See you round too, sis.
Well, Sydney, you've been a treat.
Now get me the fuck outta here.

So, I have to wait for an hour and *if* my guitar
doesn't turn up then they'll send it on when it
does…. Brilliant.

Useless tour manager has yet to phone through with any details about my transport here.

I hate this city already.

I no longer need coffee.

I need something much stronger.

Time check — 7.58.

Check in counter is over there —

WHOOOOOA! I am NOT standing in that queue. Is it even moving?

When's the gate open?

9.55. Stacks of time.

Grab a coffee. Finish this letter.

CHAPTER FOUR

EIGHT AM

Seven bucks for a coffee? Yeeeeeah, nah, I think I'll sit this one out thanks.

Guess I'll grab this seat...

Where's that note pad?

OK, so what to write... what to write... drawing a blank.

Hmmm, airports are always full of all these lonely people.

Where do they come from? Where do they belong?

Wow! That girl over there is very cute.

Like top shelf cute.

Rocking a pair of Chuck All Stars, those baby's in black. A certifiable classic. Nice choice.

And a guitar too. Instantly hot. How's that Ryan Adams song go...

"English girls are pretty when they play guitar."

Wonder if she's English?

Nah, doesn't look it.

Who's she with?

No one.

If only you wore glasses Mystery Guitar Girl, I think you'd be my perfect woman.

Was that a smile?

Did she just... smile at me?

...Oh.... no.

OK, come on Grant, stop procrastinating and finish this letter. Let's try one last time.

"Abigail, I'm so sorry for... everything...

and... and......

... aaaaaaaaaaaand especially this letter which is rubbish and I can't write to save my life and I hate writing and GAHHAHHHHH"

One of life's most under-valued pleasures, destroying paper with garbage you've written on it.

Alright, enough of that, I guess I'll write her something when I get there. May as well get back to my book instead, that queue doesn't seem to have eased off any. Come on Mr Salinger, inspire me with your wisdom... Franny & Zooey my old friends, what do you have to teach me today... what page was I on again... fifty-six me thinks. Ah yep...

'Franny quickly tipped her cigarette ash, then brought the ashtray an inch closer to...'

Wait, what's mystery guitar girl doing?

Is she?

She is! She just reached into that woman's duty-free bag and stole her vodka.

Wow, that's gutsy. Ten out of ten for having the balls to do that. Bravo.

Oh, and she's putting a fifty in the bag. Good work, nice thinking.

It's the perfect crime, from the almost perfect

woman.

And they are off, and she's in the clear. I salute you ma'am!

Ugh, did that weird guy over there see me do that?

Great, he's probably gonna narc on me given the morning I've had.

Worry about that if it happens. First, I need that drink.

And crack that lid open... carefully sneak a gulp.

AHHHHHH, my lord, that's better.

Why oh why do you make everything better alcohol?

'Excuse me, is that your bottle of vodka?'

Gulp.

'Pardon?'

'Is that your bottle? It's just that I left my bag here a moment ago and it had a bottle of that very same vodka in it and now it's gone. And I believe you have stolen it.'

Oh god, now I've done it.

'It's... it was...'

Great Nina, well bloody done. Straight to jail before you've even set foot in Sydney.

Hope this effort at spontaneous chivalry is worth it Grant...

'Here we go my love, two cups as requested.'

'Thanks...?'

'Who are you?'

'I'm her husband.'

'Really?

'Oh yes, we're newlyweds. We're on our honeymoon.'

Don't push it Grant.

'Hmmmm, well your *wife* has stolen my bottle of vodka.'

'You mean this bottle?'

'Yes, she stole that from me.'

'No, she didn't steal this.'

'She did!'

'No, it's mine.'

'Yours?'

'Yes, you see my wife's pregnant so obviously, wouldn't touch a drop. She was simply minding it while I grabbed some cups for a drink. Thank you darling. They were all out of Evian though.'

'Oh, not to worry.'

'So, who's the other cup for then?'

'Huh?'

'The other cup? Who's it for if she's pregnant?'

'No one.'

'Then why did you need to get two?'

Damn it, think Grant, think!!

'Ha! If you only knew the morning I've had.'

Annnnnd great... I've brought this upon myself. On the morning I finally decided to quit drinking for good, here I am knocking back double shots of voddy to save some girl I've never met from going to jail.

'Well, I don't think that's what happened at all, and I'm going to get the police—

'UURRGGHHHHH.'

'My god, darling are you OK?'

'My... ulcer....'

'The doctor said to not get stressed! Oh god. Doctor! Is anyone here a doctor? Come on darling. We'll find someone.'

'Ugh, OK. Get my bags. And the guitar.'

'OK, we're terribly sorry. I hope your vodka turns up.'

And now I'm running from the scene of a crime with a petty thief, who at least has great taste in footwear.

'Thanks. For helping with that.'

'There was a time I'd have done worse for a drink.'

'That was some pretty quick thinking back there though. Least I can do is offer you a proper drink. To thank you.'

'No, that's OK.'

'Please. I insist.'

…I guess detox starts tomorrow Grant.

'There's a few chairs over by the window.'

'OK. Here's your bags.'

'Thanks. Here you go. Cheers.'

'So, apart from the excellent five finger discount shopping opportunities, what brings you to the rear end of the world?'

'I'm performing at the festival tonight.'

'I guess the guitar should have been a giveaway that you're a musician of some type. So, is it really a world of hand-picked brown M & M's?'

'Nah, yellow ones are my poison. Love those little fuckers.'

'So... ahhh, is this dog-eared, heavily

bookmarked and generally mistreated copy of "Lonely Planet's Guide to Sydney" yours?'

'A friend in Tokyo gave it to me.'

'You know they say most of the stuff in these is written by people who've never been to half the places.'

'Never let the truth get in the way of a good story.'

'Is that where you came from? Tokyo?'

'Yes, I was performing there last night, now onto the Australian leg of the tour.'

'Where's your entourage?'

'I'm far from that important. Just me and a couple of guitars travelling the world.'

'Right.'

'What's that?'

'What?'

'That book you're coyly trying to conceal from my view.'

'It's nothing.'

'Give it here. Come on.'

'OK.'

'"Franny & Zooey" huh. Looks like it ain't the first time you've read this — the spine is barely held together. Any good?'

'It's OK.'

'Wow with a rave review like that I must at least check it out... open at a random page and see... hmmmm "*I like to ride in trains too much...*".

'"*You never get to sit near the window when you're married*"'.

'So you HAVE read it then.'

'Sarcasm. That's novel. We don't get much of that round these parts.'

'Salinger huh? Never got the attraction. Holden Caulfield was a whiny little prat.'

'The greatest anti-hero ever created!'

'Hardly.'

'Oh, sorry, I didn't realise you're culturally bankrupt.'

'Oh, please. I'll see your Caulfield and raise you a Huck Finn and a Patrick Bateman, at least.'

Holden, whiny! I need a drink to calm me after that.

'Refill?'

'Sure. So, you're a local?'

'Yeah, well, was. I'm saying a long overdue "adios" Sydney, and I am not looking back.'

'It's that good here, huh?'

'Leave a trail of breadcrumbs to the departure gate and you'll love it.'

'Where are you heading?'

'Amsterdam. To start with anyway.'

'So level with me Local, is The Rocks really the "must see" destination this book says it is?'

'The Rocks, The Opera House, Darling Harbour, the City, the inner west, the north shore, the Bridge, avoid them all.'

'Have you considered a career as a tour guide? What about Bondi?'

'Good god no.'

'That's a shame. It's the only place that I really needed to visit.'

'A Brit in Bondi, I'll alert the media.'

'You finished your drink? Want another?'

'Would be rude not to I guess. So, tell me Guitar Girl, why're you getting tanked so early?'

'Long story.'

'Bore me.'

'Airline lost my guitar. Ride hasn't shown. Boyfriend dumped me.'

'You weren't lying when you said it was a long story.'

She's got a great smile... and amazing, really soulful, "I'm-a-huge-bag-of-trouble" eyes.

Whoa, how much have I drunk now?

Is that five shots of vodka now, or six?

Or seven?

'So, Local, why the lost love for Sydney?'

'It's not one particular thing — we've both sucked enough life out of each other. It's just time to move on, get some space from one another. Sometimes you just gotta say "hey it's not you, it's me".'

'Think you're pretty cute, don't you?'

'I go alright.'

'When did you last get laid?'

Where did that come from?!

'When was the last time *you* got laid?'

'Couple of nights ago.'

'Last night.'

'Liar.'

'Why would I need to lie to you? I'm never gonna see you again.'

'Ideal opportunity for complete honesty then Local, no?'

That was an unexpected line of questioning.

It calls for another shot.

Whoops, that's a big glassful.

... this is fun.

'You got a sharp dress sense Local — your mother should know better than to let you leave the house like that?'

This just became not fun. Very quickly.

'Whoa, would you look at the time, I've gotta go check into my flight.'

'Righty-o.'

'It's been real.'

'No problem. Thank you, for... back there.'

It's funny how you can go from liking someone a whole bunch one second to wanting to be as far from them as possible the next with just one comment.

'Good luck with your show.'

'Good luck with life.'

Oh, he's left his book behind!

'Wait, hey wait up mystery Sydney grumpy guy, you left your book!'

Where has he gone?

Can I see him?

...Nope, he's gone.

Hmmm, well, I guess I just scored a copy of "Franny & Zooey" then.

Time to get outta here now anyway.

Guess I'll head to the taxi stand and make my own way into town. Thanks a bunch, Sydney A&R guy.

Alright Taylor, calm down.

Things can't get any worse... surely.

I'm not drunk.

I'm definitely not drunk.

I'm definitely *definitely* not drunk.

                  ... I definitely can't look like I'm drunk.

Walk in a straight line.

That's it, you're doing fine. No one will suspect a thing.

Just join the queue, check in, and get the flock through the departure gate.

Has my bag gotten heavier?

Definitely not drunk.

Why is that woman giving me stares?

What's her problem?

Oh, I'm stepping on her bag

'Sorry.'

Definitely not drunk.

Did someone turn up the heat in here?

OK, we're getting to the front of the line.

One more and—

'ARGGHH!'

CRASH, WHACK, DINGGGGG.

Who put that there?!

Stupid metal ballast thingy tripping me up.

'You OK sir?'

'Yesth, I'm good. I just tripped on the... the thing.'

Did that sound drunk?

'Do you need a hand getting up?'

'I. Am fine.'

OK, that sounded drunk.

Great, that desk is open. Walk cool Grant.

Not drunk, not drunk.

'Hiya!'

Oops, think I slammed that passport down too hard.

'Sorry.'

'Just a moment sir.'

Where's she walking off to?

Why is she talking to that security guard?

Act sober, act sober, act sober. Here he comes.

'Is this your passport sir?'

Why isn't my mouth working? Just nod, you stupid head.

'Come with me please.'

'Bud my fly-ight.'

'Come with me please sir.'

'An I getting am upgrade?'

That definitely sounded drunk.

I think I'm drunk.

'BUT I'M NOT DRUNK!'

'Sir, our staff have deemed you a flight risk and we can not allow you to fly today.'

'Just give me some water! Coffee, I'll be fine. I'm not even that drink — drunk.'

'How did you get so hammered this early?'

'Wasn't my fault.'

'Never is.'

'Barry?'

'What the fuck was that?'

'The intercom, and stop swearing in my office. Yes, Pam?'

'That's a code 567 clearance there.'

'Thanks Pam. OK Mr Ryder, now you're definitely not flying today, but if you sober up and come back tomorrow —'

'For fuck sake.'

'*IF* you sober up, we can transfer you onto the same flight tomorrow.'

'Fantastic.'

'The transfer fee though as we are now within a twenty-four-hour period for that is... let me see, four hundred and seventy eight dollars.'

'Oh come on. I'm fine. Just let me fly.'

'Airline policy. Or you can forfeit the flight entirely.'

'Look, look OK, I was a little tipsy, but I'm fine. Please...'

Breath Grant, just breath and plead your case.

'Look, I can't be here in this city. Not today.'

'Why?'

'I just... can't.'

'What have you done?'

'Nothing.'

'Is someone after you? Are you in trouble?'

'No.'

'So, you've done nothing and no one is after you?'

'Yes. I mean no. I mean yes no one is after me and I've haven't done anything. I just... can't. Personal reasons.'

'I have something for you....'

YES! I think he's going to help me. Thank you, Jesus!

'...now where is it, where is it. Ahh here we go.'

'What's this?'

'Tell me what you see?'

'Directions to a hardware store.'

'Exactly. Go and set yourself up with a bag of cement and harden up son. We'll see you in twenty four hours. Sober!'

Four hundred and ninety bucks. Most expensive drink I've ever had. Thank you girl I'll never see again. Great, so that leaves me a grand total of... what's this receipt say?

Great, eighty four dollars left in my account.

Well ain't that just the perfect amount of moolah to start a new life... baby, you're a rich man...

FARK!

Fark fark farkity fark.

Alright, well what am I gonna do?

Time check — 8.49.

Options.

Hang out at the airport for a day?

No. I'm not one of those people.

I doubt Emily's gonna want to pick me up.

Really don't want to hang out in the city.

Wonder if Dave still needs help on that chaperone job. Best shove my tail between my legs and give him a call I guess.

'Dave, hi it's Grant. So, umm... things have changed and I was wondering if maybe you still needed help on that job you mentioned this morning? Is it still open? Oh yeah. Actually, could you come get me? From the airport? It's a long story. No, I'm fine. I'll be on my best behaviour. I promise. OK. Thanks, I'll see you soon.'

Lemons to lemonade, lemons to lemonade.

Look at those planes taking off... that should be me up there.

Fuck.

CHAPTER FIVE

NINE AM

'Where are your bags?'

'I threw 'em in a locker at the storage place in the terminal. Figured it's easier than lugging them all over town til tomorrow.'

'I still can't believe you got kicked off your flight. Actually wait, it's *you*, of course I can believe it happened.'

'It wasn't my fault. Seriously.'

'Someone magically plied you with alcohol?'

There's no use arguing, it's as ridiculous as it sounds.

'Anyway Dave, thanks for picking me up.'

'Thank you for getting me out of a bind.'

'So tell me about the job, who am I looking after, how many are there?'

'Have a look in the folder. On the back seat.'

'This blue one?'

'Yeah, that's the one.'

'You've got to be joking.'

'What?'

'I'm not doing this job.'

'Why not?!'

'Unless I'm seriously mistaken, it's a bunch of clowns.'

'They're not clowns, give it here —'

'— Eyes on the road!'

'Calm down. They're not clowns, they're performers.'

'Who perform in a circus.'

'Not necessarily.'

'They're clowns.'

'They're hilarious, they'll have you in stitches, so I'm told. Come on, help me out.'

'Fine. But I need to be paid upfront.'

'Nope, you know the deal. I'm already paying you double —'

'TRIPLE!'

'Fine, I'm already paying you triple, you have to do the job first, then get paid, just like everyone else.'

'But I need some money, per diems at least. I've nothing on me and there's like four of them. How am I gonna pay for anything?'

'I've only got the company card.'

'That'll do nicely.'

'You're dreaming.'

'You never give me your money.'

'I'll pull over at petrol station and get some cash out then.'

'Fine. I think your phone's ringing.'

'Thanks. I'll put it on speaker, so I need you to keep it down.'

'Yes sir!'

'Thanks. Revolver Touring, Dave speaking.'

'Dave, hi, this is Nina Taylor.'

'Oh hi Nina, I am so so so sorry I missed your arrival, there was a mix up with the itineraries, I won't go into it, but I'm so very sorry. I just literally left the airport.'

'It's OK, I just got a taxi from the airport, and I'm at the hotel now.'

'OK great, well I'm just sorting out one last job then I will head right over to the hotel.'

'Actually, that's why I'm calling, I'm going to be fine to get myself around today, so I was ringing to say don't worry about coming over. I just want to lay low today. I'm only sleeping, well that's the plan.'

'Yeah, sure I can understand that, but I really need to pop over to see you for a while, still some things to arrange to make sure you get to the show. Look I won't be long, thirty minutes' tops, just relax, order some room service, watch some Netflix and I'll see you shortly.'

'Sure. OK, see you then.'

'OK bye.'

'Was that this Nina? On this comp card at the back of your folder.'

'Huh, pass it here. Ahhhh yeah, that's her.'

'OHHHHH, I am taking that job.'

'No way, she is a major client, you can't handle this one. Not after what you pulled last time. And especially not after the mix up this morning, I have to make sure she's properly looked after the rest of the day.'

'I'm taking that job.'

'No Grant.'

'Fine, then let me out.'

'Come on Grant, don't fuck around.'

'You know I can handle it. And I'm much less likely to screw up handling one person than looking after four all day.'

'Don't use your twisted logic on me. You're not looking after Nina.'

'Give me that job or I'm walking. I'm serious.'

'GRRRRRRR, fine! You petulant fucking child. But DON'T fuck it up.'

'Oh, I won't. And I still need money. Now.'

'I'm gonna regret taking your call, aren't I?'

KNOCK KNOCK KNOCK.

'Hold on, I'm coming.'

I gotta record this moment, the look on her face will be worth it.

'Surprise!'

'Wh... what are you doing here? Shouldn't you be halfway to, where was it again?'

'Amsterdam. But ask me why I'm here.'

'Why are you here?'

'Funny story actually, OHH, no wait, NOT so funny, I was kicked off my flight for being intoxicated.'

'HAHAHAHAHAHAHA, no really, why are you here?'

'I'm serious, you got me drunk, and I was kicked off my flight.'

'I didn't get you drunk.'

'Semantics, but it's true. Saving your petty theft antics resulted in me missing my flight.'

'Oh, in that case, I'm sorry for laughing, but why are you *here* here?'

'I guess the Lord works in mysterious ways, or to be more precise Dave from Revolver does.'

'Oh right. Well, I told him I was fine to look after myself today so, thanks for stopping by but I really don't need a babysitter. I'd prefer to just do my own thing. But thank you.'

'Look — I've been told to show you the sights; make sure you stay out of trouble. That's all OK, the day's yours.'

'I don't need anyone to hold my hand.'

'I don't wanna hold your hand. This ain't ideal for me either. I was set to be anywhere but this damned city today but now I need to do this job and show you around so I can get the money to get outta here. We can work it out, can't we? Please. It is kinda your fault that I'm here anyway.'

'What time is it?'

'Nine forty.'

By the look on her face, I think I'm winning her over.

'Alright, just wait here a minute.'

'OK.'

Bingo. I have won her over.

'Look Local, I'm sorry you missed your flight. I really hope you make the next one. Until then, take these as an apology. Goodbye.'

'Hey!'

Bottles from the mini bar to apologise? Seriously?

Fine, I guess plan B it is then.

'Excuse me... Darren?'

'Good morning good morning Miss Taylor, how can I help you?'

'Oooh, you're very chipper.'

'Just my way of getting through the day.'

'If I wanted to get a great view of Sydney, like the postcard type one, where's the best place to go?'

'Do you want to know a secret?'

'Sure.'

'Well if you want the best view, a bird's eye view, you could try the Observation Tower, it's just over the road.'

'And the harbour? How far is that?'

'You can walk it in about ten, fifteen minutes. Would you like a map?'

'No, I'm happy to just get lost exploring. Thanks.'

'No problem Miss Taylor. Any time at all. And thank you for choosing the QT.'

Well, after the shower and the purge, I feel ten pounds lighter. As good a day as any to take this new bag for a stroll.

OK, so Observation Tower huh, let's see what you got Sydney.

CHAPTER SIX

TEN AM

OK, all I have to do is keep following at a safe distance, just make sure she doesn't see me, and ensure she stays out of harm's way.

Hold up, who this guy approaching her?

Oh, another *fan* wanting a photo. Guess she must be kinda famous then... wish I had some idea who she is. Or at least what her music's like.

Mental note — Google her when you find WIFI.

Now, where is she? Focus Grant.... OK, where's she going?

The Museum of Contemporary Art huh. I can do a bit of culture I guess.

Is this creepy? Following her around like this?

Undoubtedly.

If only this were a rom-com, it would be perfectly acceptable behaviour.

No, I've become a fully blown stalker.

Have I? Not really, I mean I have an assignment. Like a private eye.

Yeah, I'm a private eye.

Or a private security guard keeping watch over her.

I bet that's what the real stalker weirdos tell themselves too.

This is too creepy. I should stop.

No concentrate, you need to do this, to get her to the gig, to get paid.

It's work, nothing more. Nothing less.

Oh, where's she gone now?

Around this corner?

Nope.

Over in that room?

Damn it.

Where is she? Back there...no.

Great! I've lost her.

Fucking brilliant Grant.

Idiot.

I'll wait out the front, she's bound to head to the exit at some point, I'll catch her as she leaves.

Unless she's already gone.

Quick, run.

'Sorry, excuse me, pardon me, sorry.'

Get out of my way. Stalking weirdo coming through.

Is she out here? Why are there so many tourists today of all days?

What was she wearing?

Clothes. Great, top shelf private eye you are Grant, can't even remember what she was wearing.

Is that her?

I think that's her.

No.

Damn it!

DING DING DING

'Look out mate!'

Uhhhh.

Ouch.

'FUCKING CYCLIST! You're all menaces! You can't just knock people down in the street!'

'Need a hand up?'

It's her.

Hooray.

I mean, oh shit though, it's her!

She knows I've been following her.

'Bloody bike lanes. They keep popping up when you least want 'em.'

'Answer something for me, how are you supposed to make sure I stay out of harm's way if you can't avoid it yourself?'

'Well if you'll stop fannying around and let me do my job—'

'—Excuse me I just saved your hide back there.'

'And who's at fault for putting me in a potentially life threatening situation?'

'A bike was about to mow you down, it hardly counts as life threatening.'

'We'll agree to disagree.'

'I'm not going to shake you, am I?'

'Nope. And it would really make stalking you a lot easier if I could do it within this general ten-foot vicinity. Come on, I really need the money for this job.'

'*IF* we do this, no bitching if I want to do the touristy stuff.'

'As long as I get you to your soundcheck on time so I can get paid, Sydney's your clam. Look, I get that you want to be alone. There's nothing better than exploring a new city on your own. But I promise I'll leave you to have your space. You won't see me. You'll barely hear a peep out of me all day if you don't want.'

'Promise?'

'Promise.'

'Alright then Local, let's do this. Lead the way.'

'By the way, I'm Grant, and I'll be your tour guide for the day.'

'I think I prefer "Local" Local.'

'Suit yourself boss.'

I agree to let him show me around... and now he goes all silent.

This is going to be a long day.

Ugh, I've never wanted to be home more than I do right now.

How many days away is it?

Let's see.... I left in October, so that's... three... and a half months.

I miss it so much right now.

I wonder what Megan's doing tonight? I wonder how her shop's doing? If she finally got the place open?

Just one more thing I missed while being on the road...

'So... what do you want to do?'

'You're the local, Local, why don't you tell me what's worth seeing.'

'Well it's Saturday, sun's out. The beach?'

'I've seen enough beaches lately. What would you suggest doing?'

'Doesn't bother me, so long as I don't have to see

anyone I know. Or have to pat a fucking koala. Otherwise, whatever you want.'

This is gonna be painful....

'So I ahhh, saw a few people wanting to have photos with you.'

'You saw that?'

'Sorry. Was just trying to...'

'Do a job, yeah I get it.'

'So, you're pretty famous?'

'If you're hoping this'll turn into some sort of "Notting Hill" experience, you'll have to aim a little higher up the celebrity food chain. I mean I have one song that's kinda done alright. It's getting me some attention I guess.'

'What's it like?'

'The song?'

'The attention. And the song.'

'The attention is.... weird. Nice, but it still jolts me when someone steps into my face and acts like they know me. They're mostly chilled, but there's been the occasional drunken jerk.'

'And the song?'

'You can hear it later at the show.'

'Influences?'

'Emmylou, Joni, Dolly, Stevie—'

'Wonder?'

'Nicks. And a bit of Alanis.'

'Interesting.'

'How?'

'Just that you said all your influences are women.'

'That's just who's music I respond to most. It's not an agenda.'

'I didn't mean it like that.'

'How did you mean it?'

'Never mind.'

Let's curb that conversation before it gets outta hand.

Awkward silence settles in again....

'Hey Local.'

'What?'

'D'you hear what happened when they recently started showing the Flintstones in the United Arab Emirates?'

'No. What?'

'Well they don't really like it in Dubai, but the people in Abu Dhabi do.'

Nothing.

Not even a smile.

'That's champagne comedy right there, bub.'

'Meh.'

Give me strength.

'Oooooh, let's get on one of those red buses.'

'No way, they're full of tourists and a complete rip-off.'

And this is where I introduce my foot to your shin.

Hard.

'OWWWW, the fuck you do that for?'

'I said no whining. Come on.'

'See, this is great fun!'

'Doesn't take much to please some people I guess.'

'OK Local, lay it on me, what's with the Sydney malevolence?'

'It's all so fucking lame — the Opera House, the Bridge, Taronga Zoo, the ferry to Manly. Only takes a day, tops, to see it all. A two-hundred-year history that's bred less culture than a tub of yoghurt.'

'I think you're seeing it with tired eyes.'

'Yeah OK, there's some cultural cringe, but it's not just that. Everything is just so bloody expensive, taxis, food, seven bucks for a coffee?! And entertainment, what little there is.'

'You do know Amsterdam's one of the most expensive cities in the world? And it's overrun with bicycles too come to think of it.'

'Everyone in Sydney is so obsessed with real estate — where do you live, how much did that cost, did you have a better broker than us? The city is practically deserted by six on a weeknight as everyone rushes to the home they can't even afford. For the average earner, there's little chance of ever owning your own place here anyway then add to that the rent is off the charts. Stop me at any time if I'm ranting.'

'By all means, get it all out.'

'Oh, and the conversations — christ, if it's not real estate, it's how much we lost at the TAB last weekend.'

'Me thinks the lady doth protest too much — it's hardly poverty stricken, war torn or structurally undemocratic.'

'Well that's it — there's nothing fundamentally wrong; the main problem's become the people.'

'I'm beginning to see why.'

'I don't think there is another group of people on the planet who collectively whine louder or more often than Sydneysiders.'

'And you call us Poms "whingers".'

'Next stop is World Square, folks. World Square is the next stop.'

'Exactly! It's hardly surprising given it's become a complete nanny state. There's absolutely no nightlife anymore thanks to the draconian pseudo-Christian drinking laws. But even the little things that made the city great are getting ruined.'

'Such as?'

'Every day at dusk thousands of bats used to fly across the sky, from the Botanic Gardens to Centennial Park. Thousands, and for over an hour. It looked amazing.'

'Sounds beautiful.'

'But these NIMBYS—'

'NIMBYS?'

'Not In my Back Yard's, residents with nothing better to do than complain, anyway they decided the bats were destroying vegetation, so the council started to fire out ultrasonic sounds from the park to drive them away. People in this city need to get some perspective on where they fit in the world.'

'My latte's leaking, the beach is too crowded, the bats are missing from my sky. Cry baby cry.'

'Exactly. I'm your archetypal whinging Sydneysider... and that's why I've gotta get out of here. I've become what I hate. There's gotta be something better out there. Something I've gotta get into my life. Figure I'll follow the sun til I find it.'

'You need to chill Local. I think we're going to do some stuff today you wouldn't normally do. And to help facilitate that, you're going start by scoring us some weed.'

'Yeah, that's not gonna happen.'

'Really?'

'Yes really.'

'OK see you later.'

'Where are you going?'

'I really don't know Local. Who knows where I'll end up. Guess it will be up to you to explain why I became a headline in tomorrow's newspaper. 'Talented, and more than a wee bit glamorous, English musician Nina Taylor went missing, presumed having a great time, whilst she was meant to be under the watchful eye of a scurrilous local tour guide. The manhunt continues...'

'Point taken.'

'Being?'

'That I'm your bitch.'

'That's the spirit.'

'So you want weed?'

'We need weed.'

'I sense I won't get through today without a criminal record.'

'If it all goes to plan.'

Time check — 10.35.

Right, who do I know with weed?

I could try Bill, he usually has something. Haven't spoken to him in ages though. Is it weird to call him out of the blue? One way to find out.

'Bill, it's Grant. Yeah, been a while. I'll be quick. Do you have anything? OK, and are you still in Bondi? In Manly now. OK, text the address. Thanks. Bye.'

'Well?'

'That was far too easy. But you're in luck, your

life of crime can continue.'

'Goody. I love it when a plan comes together.'

'But we need to get back to Circular Quay to catch a ferry to Manly.'

'Double goody!'

'My gosh, this harbour is incredible!'

'I guess. I went to school just over there, see that red brick building with the cross on it. To the right of the bridge.'

'Ohhhh yeah. That was your school?!'

'Uh huh. I spent every day for ten years daydreaming out those windows of better places. It's all a little wasted on me now.'

'Is your glass always half empty?'

'Guess so.'

'Come on local, it's time to step up the chaperoning. So tell me a story. Expand my horizons.'

'Hmmm do you want the tourist rundown?'

'Whatever you've got.'

'OK well, you see the Opera House?'

'Kinda hard to miss.'

'Well apparently the sails, if combined, would form a perfect sphere. The architect was inspired to create it while eating an orange. That's what I'd heard anyway. And in the concert hall, there's a grand organ that has over 10,000 pipes. And each one is individually named.'

'Really? After what?'

'Musicians and technicians mainly. Though one had a particularly unfortunate name of "Fagott", unless it's a cruel nickname and phallic inanimate objects are not immune from homophobic slurs either. The pub trivia the human brain retains huh?'

'I can't get over how beautiful this harbour is.'

'It has its moments. Do you want to sit over there?'

'Sure.'

'So... what did she do?'

'Who?'

'The girl you're running away from?'

'What makes you think it's a girl?'

'OK, the boy you're running away from.'

I guess that death stare means he's not into guys. It was an each way bet.

'I don't buy the 'Fear and Loathing in Sydney' bit Local. There's more to it. And moving as far as possible from your life is quite the grand sweeping gesture of a hopeless romantic, no?'

'If you say so.'

'So what did she do?'

'A girl was involved. But that's not the main reason.... It's a long story.'

'Let's start at the end and work back. Who ended it?'

'I don't want to talk about it.'

'Guess it's gonna be a pretty long day sitting here in silence.'

Hmmm, hmmm, hmmmmmm hmmm hmmmmmm hmmmmmmmmmmmmm.

'She did.'

'Sorry?'

'She ended it.'

'What's her name?'

'Abi. Abigail.'

'Why?'

'Cause that's her name.'

'No, why did it end?'

This is like pulling teeth.

'OK, give me three guesses.'

OK, let's think... I know, I'll mime her walking in on him with another girl.

No.

With another man.

Nope.

She walks in on him trying on her clothes.

'It just ended OK. Some things just do.'

'And you miss her huh?'

'No. Maybe.... I don't know. I suppose so. It's just that eventually everything became... not good enough. Didn't take the correct wine to parties, never had enough money. She even complained about the way I ordered food at a Chinese restaurant. It actually ended two days after that fight. I think my relationship ended because of sweet and fucking sour pork. So that stuff, no, I don't miss... But you know, sure I guess there are things I miss.'

'Such as?'

'Stupid stuff.'

'Misery loves company. I just got dumped this morning too.'

'I miss... I miss sleeping with her.'

'The sex?'

'No. Not just that. Just the sleeping. Some people just... fit... right... next to each other... and the little things... But I don't know if I miss her anymore or just miss having someone. A "you".'

'A me?'

'No, a "you"... the one that lives in all the songs and books.'

'.... Wow. She really did a number on you, didn't she?'

And now we're back to him doing his best Marcel Marceau impression.

I know, I'll soften him with one of my astoundingly great dad jokes... let's see which one... Ahhh, yes!

'Hey Local, where would you find a one legged dog?'

'I don't know, where?'

'Same place you left him.'

Nothing? Really?!

He is one tough nut to crack.

CHAPTER SEVEN

ELEVEN AM

KNOCK KNOCK KNOCK.

'Who is it?'

'Grant.'

'Hold on a second.'

He seems to be making a lot of noise in there.

Did he just step on a cat then?

… Finally.

'Hey Bill. Thanks for helping out with—'

'—Who's she? I told you to come alone man. This is not cool. Not fucking cool at all.'

'She's OK, she's with me. Her name's Nina. She's just a tourist, a friend I know.'

'Bonjour.'

'Wait — aren't you.... Nina Taylor? Is that you?'

'Yes, it is.'

'Oh my god! Haha, what the fuck are you doing at my house?'

'I was hoping to borrow a cup of sugar but failing that we were hoping you could help us out with some weed.'

'Oh shit, I can't believe it. We're going to your show tonight, my... ahhh girl, she loves you, plays your stuff non-stop. Nina Fucking Taylor! She'll never believe it. Hang on a sec, I need to get my camera.'

'This happen often?'

'Only on dodgy drug runs in foreign countries.'

'Here, Grant take a picture. Press there. Yeah, that one.'

'Say "I love Sydney".'

'Cheese.'

'And done.'

'Thanks. Wow. Oh here's what you wanted Grant.'

'Thanks very much. Here's the cash.'

'Actually here, a second one on me.'

'Muchos gracias señor Bill.'

'So how do you two know each other?'

'I have—'

'—It's all a bit of a blur, right Local?'

'Right.'

'I heard or I thought I heard you were leaving town or something?'

'Supposedly. One day. Loving the new bungalow Bill, been here long?'

'No, about six months.'

'Right. Anyway, sorry again about the early call.'

'S'all right, especially for Nina Taylor. Still can't believe it. Ohhhh, I think that's the phone inside.'

'You go grab it, and we'll head off. Thanks mate.'

'Thanks so much Bill, see you at my show.'

'You bet, front and centre. Bye Grant.'

'He was a nice guy.'

'You have an interesting definition of "nice", obviously. He serves a purpose, but I have no desire to spend any more time than absolutely necessary in his company.'

Back to the silent treatment, huh?

Dooo dooooo deeee daaah doo doo dee dah doooo.

'I'm gonna put some music on if you're gonna keep hitting mute on me.'

'Sorry, I'm just... mulling stuff over.'

'Thinking about where you should be right now?'

'That. And other things.'

'Have you got the lighter we bought?'

'Here you go.'

And inhale....

...

....AAHHHHHHH.

That's better.

'Pass it here. Thanks.'

'Well, I'm really not a fan of silence so...'

'You're not, are you? All morning you've been "tell me a story", "what are you thinking?", clicking your tongue, making weird noises and talking to yourself.'

'I don't talk to myself.'

Do I?

'And so what if I do?"

'Ha.'

'What?'

'No, nothing.'

'WHAT!'

'I bet you ten bucks you couldn't last thirty seconds in complete silence.'

'Don't be stupid. I can go days without speaking to someone.'

I don't need to talk.

I can get by without speaking.

Or making sounds or... ooooh I wonder if that's that game?

'Is that AFL those kids are playing over there?'

'Told you.'

'Told me what?'

'That you couldn't last thirty seconds.'

'Well if you'd told me we'd started the bet, it would have helped! Puff puff give, stop messing up the rotation. Pass it here.'

'Fine. We'll double it. Twenty bucks you can't last thirty seconds in silence.'

'Fine.'

'OK, you ready? Starting...NOW!'

He will not win.

He won't.

He can stare me down all he wants.

Means nothing.

I will not cave in.

I will not.

Will not.

WILL NOT!!!

'AHHHHHHH, OK, fine, I hate silence!! It's annoying and makes me feel self-conscious and awkward.'

'Twenty bucks.'

'Take it out of my rider.'

'Cheapskate.'

'I hate it. Stupid ugly horrible silence! I would literally kill myself if I went deaf. Literally. I could not handle it.'

'Deaf I could handle — I've considered ramming a knitting needle in there some days so I wouldn't have to put up with other people's bullshit. But going blind, that would ruin me.'

'But what about all the music you'd miss out on?!'

'I'd rather be able to watch films, and read books, see art... look at porn — nah, I couldn't trade music for all that.'

'I'd happily trade all those for every piece of music in the world.'

'Music and I have a bit of a love/hate relationship anyway, so there's times I can take it or leave it. Pass me the joint.'

'Really! Why?'

'Well, you know, with all the baggage it comes with. I can't tell you how many times I've had to drag myself back down 'Abbey Road' after some girl almost ruined it forever when it accompanied her "why we need to break up" speech.'

'There should be an unspoken rule — if you're gonna break up with someone, there should definitely be no music playing.'

'Agreed. You want the last of this?'

'Sure.'

'Right, well what do you want to do now?'

'What do you do for fun in Sydney?'

'Well there's the beaches, and bars and—'

'No, what do YOU do for fun? There's gotta be one thing that only you like to do. What's a day in the life of the Local entail?'

'Well... there's... one thing. But you'll probably think it's stupid.'

'Let me be the judge of that. Is it far?'

'No, it's maybe five blocks away.'

'You thought I'd think this was stupid? That you're into archery?'

'It's not your typical hipster hobby. So you don't mind?'

'Not at all.'

'You done it before?'

'It'll be a first.'

'OK, I'll show you how to do it. I'll just rent one range. Hey Tony.'

'Grant! It's been a while mate.'

'Ah yeah, I was injured. Can I rent one and two sets?'

'Here you go, why don't you take range five.'

'Thanks.'

'How long have you been doing this?'

'About fifteen years. On and off.'

Well isn't this boy full of surprises!

'OK, so take the bow like this.'

'Like this?'

'No, hook your index finger.'

'This?'

'No, wait let me show you. I... I'm going to get my arm around you now, OK?'

He's so adorably awkward.

'It's fine.'

'OK, now hold it like... like you've formed a "V" with your index finger and thumb. Now keep your arm locked straight, and roll your elbow out.'

'Oh I see. More like that?'

'Yeah. Now draw back. Keep your right eye closed and look directly at the bullseye. Line that mark up with the tip of the arrow. And release.'

'BULLSEYE!'

'Ha, not quite, but not bad for a first attempt. Try it yourself now.'

OK, form a V, arm locked and... release!

'I hit it!'

'You're a natural. But I wouldn't be signing up for the England Olympic team just yet though.'

'This is fun. And you thought I'd think this was stupid. Shame on you.'

'It always relaxes me.'

'OH DAMN!!'

'What?'

'I just remembered, I've gotta change my relationship status before he does.'

'Seriously? Why'd people persist with that site?'

'You're not on it?'

'Leaves me with nothing more than the overwhelming urge to shower.'

'If you don't feel dirty after using Facebook, y'aren't doing it right.'

'For someone who just got dumped, you're doing a good job concealing it.'

'I'm more annoyed that he beat me to the punch if I'm honest; the relationship was on its last legs.'

'How long did you go out?'

'Two years.'

'Was it long, short, average?'

'You boys and your hang-ups.'

'What? No! I was talking about the length of the

relationship!'

'Oh. Sorry. Ummm, Above average. By quite a bit actually. For me anyway. Could have married him, if it came up.'

'Really?'

'Yeah. Not that it would have been a great idea. At the same time, you can't hold on to something that's not really there.'

'Right.'

'Oh how the fuck do you change the settings on this stupid app!'

'Give it here. And... there, done.'

'Thanks, that was quick.'

'That's what all the girls say, sadly.'

'You look the type.'

'Thanks. So when did you know it was over?'

'In the silence.'

'It sucks when you stop having things to talk about.'

'No, it wasn't that. There was just a pause after every sentence — this empty 'thing' just hanging there, momentarily, that seemed like it might be filled with the words able to fix everything in an instant before it just fades away. When you'd rather avoid going home than to see that person, it's time to move on.'

Why am I being so open with this guy? I wouldn't tell Meg this much?! What's he doing to me?

'So anyway, how did you get into this?'

'Archery? Oh, I got into it for the same reason guys get into most things.'

'To impress girls?'

'Uh uh.'

'It's working. Nice shot! Now show me what you did just then, you arched your elbow up a little...'

'The first gig I ever went to?'

'Yep. And no lying to make it sound cooler.'

'Well, I'm sticking with Neil Diamond in the early 80's — Dad took Mum whilst she was pregnant. So that's it as it's far less embarrassing than the actual one.'

'Go on, what was it? I mean Neil Diamond is kind of embarrassing enough so if there's one that's even worse, I want to hear it.'

'No, that skeleton is staying where it is.'

'Who am I going to tell?'

'It's not who you're going to tell, but how you'll judge me for everything hereafter.'

'I won't. I promise. Go on tell me. Let the truth set you free.'

'I've never told anyone this before.'

'Do it.'

'OK, here goes... Cher.'

'Cher?'

'Yes.'

'Cher was the first concert you ever went to?'

'Yes.'

'BAHAHAHAHAHAHAHAHAHAHAHAHA HAHAHA.'

I knew I shouldn't have told her.

'OK, OK, laugh it up.'

'Did your boyfriend take you?'

'Dad wanted to see her—'

'—Did your dad's boyfriend take you?'

'Anyway, he thought it would be a fun family outing. She wore that fishnet body stocking thing she wore in the "Turn Back Time" video... if I could turn back time, I'd definitely have picked a better first gig to go to.'

'Cher.'

Note to self, don't tell her any more secrets.

'OK Local, truth or dare?'

'Umm, trick or treat?'

'No seriously, let's play truth or dare.'

'You realise neither of us is twelve years old, right? Are you gonna whip out one of those folded paper things with numbers on it next?'

'Huh?'

'You know, you lift the flaps up and it reveals your future through numbers... you know, that thing. All the girls made them in primary school.'

'I have absolutely no idea what you're talking about.'

'Whatever.'

'Fine, me first. I choose... dare!'

'So I have to think of a dare that you do?'

'Mhh hmm.'

OK, let's scan the beach for something to get her to do.

Hmmmm.... Let's see now... steal that child's ice cream. Nah, that's mean... Ummm, pull down that sign... nah, there's gotta be something?

Bingo!

'Him.'

'Who?'

'That muscle-bound surfer lying on the red towel. Go and get his number.'

'You haven't played this before have you. You're meant to suggest something that is really difficult to do.'

'Off you go then, you have five minutes.'

'Only need two, if that.'

I hope I'm right...

So... she's made her approach.

The flirting starts. Oooh, nice little flick of the hair there Nina.

Ahhh, biting her bottom lip, that's a good one.

OK, so that's ninety seconds.

She's making herself comfortable, sitting on the edge of his towel.

Brushed his knee with the back of her hand, clever, clever...

And...

Here he comes, right on cue, the second Mr-Muscle-bound-great-looking-guy enters the picture...

And... the two fellas kiss.

And she does the awkward introduction to the second guy.

And now the even more awkward exit.

Oooh, a little stumble as she stands up.

And here she comes, walking back, fuming...

...and here she is.

'So... do you want five more minutes?'

'Fine, you win that round.'

'Rule number one about Sydney men — if they look too good to be true, assume they're gay.'

'I guess your heterosexuality is assured then. This from a man whose first concert was Cher.'

'Let's move past that, shall we?'

'Fine, gloves are off. Truth or dare?'

'Ahhhhh... truth.'

'Why today?'

'Huh?'

'Why was it so important that you HAD to leave Sydney today?'

'It just is. I've changed my mind, I pick dare.'

'You can't do that, that's not how you play.'

'Then let's not play.'

'GRRRRR, fine... hmmmmm, OK, Hell-o! Look over there.'

'Who?'

'The girl in the green swimsuit reading the newspaper. Go and get her digits.'

'Her?'

'Scared?'

Yes.

'Hardly.'

'OK, I'll give you ten. Wait, give me your watch to keep time.'

'Fine, but please be careful with it.'

A couple of stretches first, limber up. Waste a little time... Get a few star jumps in.

'Just go, you're wasting valuable minutes.'

'Fine. If I'm not back by Tuesday, redirect my mail.'

OK, breathe Grant... she's just a very extremely attractive girl, nothing to be awkward about.

Heart racing faster now, great.

OK, just play it cool.

'Hey.'

A smile, that's a good start.

'Nice day.'

'Yeah for once right?'

'The weather's been crazy lately hasn't it with all

the rain.'

Get off the weather you boring fuck!!!

'Have you been in the water today?'

'A bit earlier, it's warming up now.'

'Nice, nice.'

God, now where do I take it?

Great, Nina's sitting right behind her now, really could do without that added pressure.

'I'm Grant.'

'Hi Grant. Hanna.'

'Nice to meet you Hanna. So, umm, I... look, I don't know if you're seeing anyone — and by the absence of a ring on your finger I'm guessing — hoping — that you're not married either... So I was wondering and I know this is a bit forward, but maybe you know, I could, grab your phone number so I could call you at some time to hang out and go and see — or you know, get something to eat — doesn't have to be around here — or it could be, you know, whatever's good for you — I'm happy to do that too you know — Japanese or — not Japanese maybe you hate that I know some people do some love it — others... So, you know, it would be great to get your number and see you. Around. Again. You know, if you wanted to. Could be fun. At least for a while. But of course, everything is finite. Eventually, the thing you really liked about that person becomes the thing that you despise. And next thing you're spending more time spitting chips at each other than — well the good stuff — and then you end up wondering what you ever saw in that person, to begin with... so maybe we should just save each other a bucket of money, time, heartache & helter skelter and just cut to the breakup now— but I don't know. What do you say?'

Annnnnnnnd... there she goes, running away from the sociopath I am.

'Real smooth Local.'

'Was it something I said?'

'I just think... you know like... what's the point in investing all this time and energy into someone new if we're both just counting down the moments until one of us gets bored... or changes our mind.'

'That's not how most people think.'

'Is in my experience. It all only ever ends in some manifestation of heartbreak anyway, so why bother? No point in spending otherwise valuable time finding someone to love me.'

'Do you really believe that?'

'I just expect it to go wrong — never know when, but it's always there, hovering in the background. Love's for people who lack ambition anyway.'

'Mmmmmaybe that's part of the problem? Approaching any relationship with such a cynical attitude?'

'It's more practical to be cynical. Wanting things to work out is much more painful.'

'Isn't one of the greatest adventures falling in love and going into it knowing how slim the odds are that it's going to work out, but throwing caution to the wind and allowing yourself to have that hope that maybe, just maybe, it will. It's never gonna be strawberry fields forever but winning that gamble it offers would always be worth the effort.'

'To some people, I guess.'

'I think it's so sad that you've gotta hide your love away to save you from some potential fleeting hurt. The reward always outweighs the risk.'

'That's the view through your glass onion, and I've got mine.'

'Seriously though, what was the thing this girl had over you? And don't tell me "the sleeping" cause you can buy pillows for that. I know cause I saw first-hand guys in Tokyo who are into that shit. Seriously. They call them "Moe", guys who develop romantic relationships with body length pillows. They get them specially designed with characters on them and everything. Some get married to them.'

'Takes all sorts.'

'Anyway, go on. What's this spell she's got you under?'

'You want me to name something I miss?'

'Yeah.'

'Ummm.... OK well, the conversation.'

'What about it?'

'We could just talk for hours and hours, about nothing and yet still find ways to keep the conversation going until the early hours.'

'Ok, so once she left your life, who filled that need?'

'What do you mean?'

'Who did you talk with for hours until the sun came up after she left?'

'You want me to name them?'

'For the love of god, YES!'

'Well... for a while, my mate Marco.'

'Who else?'

'Why?'

'Who else! Name everyone who filled that need after she left.'

'Well, I guess an old teaching mentor, Ryan... And Jay... Sarah... Jeremy and Claudia.'

'Would you say that all these people more than made up for and combined actually exceeded the ability to fill that need?'

'Yeah, but it was a different type of conversation.'

'Granted, but would you agree that you were freer to talk about certain things with these people than you could with her?'

'I guess.'

'Yes or no?'

'Yes.'

'So you see, all this great conversation you were already able to get from more than enough people in your life.'

'Well, yeah, but it wasn't just the conversation I miss.'

'I'd hope not. But if you go through and list everything that you miss about her, and apply those same questions, same comparatives, and drawbacks and missed benefits that you might see that there's nothing really to miss, cause you already had all these things in your life in another form, with other people. You just projected this need to fill it on her.'

'Perhaps, even if it's a little simplistic. A lot simplistic, actually.'

'You just gotta look at it all without the emotion

surrounding it. Emotion makes you ignorant to other possibilities. We all want someone who'll say that your heart will never be broken again. But no one can do that...'

'I know...'

'All you need is love, but that doesn't necessarily have to be the romantic kind. Hold up — I'm the one that just got dumped — why do I feel like I'm talking you off the ledge? And how did we end up at an aquarium? Having a D&M while walking through a shark tank?!'

'You wanted the touristy stuff.'

'I wanted the Sydney stuff.'

'I told you, this is about as cultured as we get.'

'I call bullshit. Anyway Local, let's get outta here. I need to smoke another joint anyway.'

'Fine. I'm intrigued where this magical mystery tour is taking us next?'

CHAPTER EIGHT

TWELVE PM

'ArghhHHHHH, I can't believe you.'

'It's true!'

'It's not fact, just opinion, and an incredibly blinkered one at that. Just... just gimme the joint you increasingly frustrating person!'

'It is! Women these days don't know what they want. You want independence but also want someone to look after you.'

'Excuse me, hold up, the problem with guys is that most aren't looking for a partner, they're looking for a mummy.'

'What's wrong with that if that's what they want. It's what women have wanted for centuries.'

'Oh please! You don't really believe this thinly veiled chauvinistic bullshit, do you?!'

'It's not, not intentionally. The thing is women pine for romance; to be swept off their feet, but they never do anything to reciprocate it. Women are about as romantic as a Dutch oven.'

'Your views are borderline offensive, but I'm

intrigued to see how deep this hole you're digging yourself will be. So go on.'

'What was the last romantic thing you did for a guy?'

'Well, I... umm... there was....'

'Exactly!'

'Wait a minute — what was the last romantic thing you did for someone?'

'Contacted her boss to arrange a surprise day off work, went horse riding in the country, champagne picnic, hotel room in the city that night and topped it off with a bracelet from Tiffany's.'

'Ok, that's pretty romantic. Cheesy as fuck, but it could be called romantic.'

'We're not adverse to romance. It's just that our expectations are so low from women that we give up. And you collectively wonder why when you can't be fucked doing it yourselves — women don't want to put in any effort.'

'Argghhh. The blanket generalisations! You're actually beginning to piss me off Local.'

'Why, cause I'm right?'

'What I wouldn't give for a large sock full of manure right now.'

'Stop quoting Woody Allen. Look —'

'— Don't tell me to 'look'!'

'I apologise. But would you agree that women today — on the whole — have their shit together?'

'Mostly, yes.'

'OK. I know way more women in our age group than men who own homes. But I also have this theory — and most guys I tell it to agree — that every woman hits an age, of around thirty, where she sees that she's got her life so together that she freaks out, not sure it's really what she wants, chucks it all in — boyfriend, job, etc. — to go and "find herself".'

'Yet another bullshit generalisation.'

'It may well be, and I can't speak with any worldly authority, but in my experience, it's true. Most guys I know are figuring out what they really what from life first rather than being pressured into what society thinks they should have achieved. And because of that, transitioning into their thirties isn't such a big deal—'

'—Yeah because they spend their time floating through that too—'

'—*because* they've already spent the time working out what they want from life. It's just that women spend their twenties doing what they think they should that once they have it, they're not sure it's what they really want.'

'Or you guys wait until your forties to freak out, fuck your secretary and buy a sports car.'

'Very possibly, but at least I've got something to look forward to.'

'If you make it that far. I'm seriously considering shortening your life expectancy after you dropped those pearls of wisdom.'

'Handbags at dawn? OK, what should we talk about next — religion or politics?'

'Either if it shuts you up. Pass me the joint.'

'Here.'

Did those two guys just give us stares as we passed them? Meh, you're being paranoid Grant. And stop pontificating with your four AM philosophy, you goose.

'Can I ask you a question?'

'What Local?'
'The Beatles?'
'What about 'em?'
'Where do you sit?'
'Down to the million-dollar question huh. Well I
—'

'Stop there you two. Inspector Kite, Manly
Police Station. My partner and I have stopped you
as we suspect you are smoking marijuana.'
Fuck.
'RUN LOCAL!'
'Huh?'
What's happening?!
'RUN FOR YOUR LIFE YOU IDIOT!'
'Go after her!'
Oh my god, am I about to do this?!
I am.
I am doing it.
I ain't sticking around for the benefit of Mr Kite
and his mate.
I'm running from the cops.
Oh god...
...*Why* am I running from the cops?!?
'Get back here! You'll only make it worse.'
What have I done?!
Oh fuck, oh fuck, oh fuck.
OH FUCKITY FUCKITY FUCK!
There's traffic coming straight at me.
'SORRY! SORRY!'
'Get off the road you stupid dickhead.'
BEEP BEEEEEEEP BBEEP
Oh shit, I'm sorry I knocked over your ice
cream little girl. I'm a terrible person.
This is fucked.

Why did I run? It's gonna be worse now...

Shit... where has she gone?

Into the ferry terminal?

Damm it, where is she?

'Down here you dummy. Quick, duck. Quiet.'

'Which way did they go? Can you see 'em?'

'I'll check down here, you go down that way.'

'OK.'

'Can you see, have the cops gone?'

'I think so.'

'Now what?'

'I don't know Local. It wasn't a fully realised plan I launched into.'

'Should we stay here? Or run back out?'

'I think that ferry at wharf three is just about to leave.'

'So?'

'So, on the count of three, run to it.'

'But we haven't got a ticket to ride it, plus it's almost left the wharf—'

'—One two THREE!'

What are we doing?! Running to jump on a moving ferry. This is insane.

Oh god, it's pulling away.

We're not gonna make it.

We're not gonna make it.

'JUMP!'

We're—

...Wow

...We, we made it.

'WOOOO! Haha, that was BRILLIANT!'

'Are you insane?!'

'I pick a moondog, so of course.'

'We're so fucked.'

'Oh come on, the most exciting thing that's happened to you all day and you're complaining.'

'Sadly, it's not and it's only— OH FUCK!'

'What?'

'I've dropped my phone. Fuck, FUCK!'

'So what?'

'So what? So all my numbers and contacts were in it!'

'You're leaving here tomorrow, so why do you care?'

'That's hardly the point.'

'You wanted a clean break from this place, no? Can't get squeakier than losing contact with everyone.'

'Em'll have a field day with this.'

'Who's Em?'

'My sister. What's gonna happen when we pull into the wharf? There'll be cops waiting there.'

'Maybe. Maybe not. Worry about that when we get there.'

'I can't be as flippant about this as you. Sorry.'

'Can I ask you something?'

'You'd do it anyway so go right ahead.'

'You want to make a fresh start. I get that. But why choose one of the most hedonistic cities in the world to clean up and start anew?'

'There's more to Amsterdam than getting wasted.'

'I know. And I agree it's a beautiful city. But why not choose somewhere that offers less temptation to fall off the rails? Kinda like a reformed gambler hoping for a change by moving to Vegas.'

'Why don't you go and see if there's an old lady round here you can mug? Seems the sort of G-rated excitement you'd revel in. And your phone is ringing.'

'I wonder who that could be?'

'Well it won't be me, will it.'

'Smartalec. Hello, Nina speaking. Oh hi Dave. Yes, he's certainly looking after me. Oh, you've been trying to call him? I think he had his phone on silent. Yes. No, we're fine. OK, yes, I'll ask him where it is. I might need to borrow a guitar though. OK great. We'll be there as soon as we can. Thanks.'

'Dave?'

'Yes. Do you know a place called the Island?'

'Sure. It's a floating pontoon someone's turned into an exclusive bar and music venue. They tow it around the harbour in summer. Why?'

'There's an artist showcase there, they had an act pull out, missed their flight or something, and wanted to know if I'd fill in for a small set.'

'Look. To be honest, I don't think I'm up for this gig. I sorted your weed. Showed you around. I'll get you to the Island, but after that, I just want to head off, do my thing and try and somehow forget that I'm stuck in this fucking place for another day. Ok?'

'But I thought you needed the money for—'

'—Excuse me you two. Can we have a word?'

Oh shit, security.

'We have a report of a couple matching your description evading police in Manly. What do you have to say about that?'

'I.. Ahh... we... you see. It was a misunderstanding, you see—'

'—MISS!! GET DOWN FROM THERE!'

Oh my god, she's standing on the edge of the ferry!

'Nina, get down! Please!'

'Come on Local, live a little.'

OH FUCK! She's jumped off the ferry!

Fuck!

'MAN OVERBOARD!'

TOOOT. TOOOOOT.

'You stay right there mate.'

'Yes sir.'

OH SHIT, OH SHIT, OH SHIT...

I can't leave her in the water, can I?

Do I really need the money this badly?!?!?

I guess I do.

' O H H H H H H H SSHHHHHHIIIIIIITTTTTTT!!!'

SPLASH!

What type of reprobate have I turned into?!

TOOOTT TOOOOOTT.

'Local! Yoo Hoo! Over here.'

'Are you fucking insane!!! What the fuck is wrong with you?! Tell me why you did that?'

'Rock n roll, Local. All in the almighty name of rock n roll!'

'The water police will nab us soon enough. That's if the sharks don't get here first.'

'Did you ever do something just for the sake of

doing it?'

'Did you ever do something with more than a second's forethought?!'

'Generally not.'

'In the short time I've known you, I've been barred from my flight, been kicked repeatedly in the shins, gotten stoned, chased by cops, lost my phone—'

'—Grown a vagina—'

'—if we do make it back to shore, we need to go our separate ways, as it won't be long before one of us — most likely me given the current chain of events — loses a limb.'

'Local, you've heard of Murphy's Law, right?'

'Yeah yeah, anything that can go wrong will.'

'But have you heard of Cole's Law?'

'What's that?'

'Thinly sliced cabbage.'

'I seriously hate you almost as much as I hate your jokes right now.'

Is that my passport floating over there?

Great.

'Ha. This waterproof bag DID come in handy. Fancy that.'

'OH WHAT THE FUCK WAS THAT!'

'Calm down local.'

'I'm serious, there's something down there!'

'Rubbish there's nothing more than an octopus's garden down there.'

'Look there's a speedboat — HEY! OVER HERE!! They're coming over.'

Great, we have to get saved by a bunch of shirtless bogans.

'WOOOOOO!!!'

'Fully sick guys.'

'Guys that was fucking incredible! We saw it all from over there.'

'Thank you, thank you, we're here every night this week and twice on Saturdays.'

'Can we give you a lift?'

'Please.'

'Yes please, and can you get us outta here quickly?'

'If there's one thing the Sun King is good for, it's quick getaways. Hold on.'

I couldn't just mind my own business in the airport this morning.

Oh no, I had to be chivalrous Grant. Fucking idiot.

What's your number one rule — KEEP TO YOURSELF!

I'm not even supposed to be here today!

'Where are we headed?'

'To The Island please.'

'Take her to the Island, but drop me at the nearest wharf. Thanks.'

'You sure?'

'Please, I'd appreciate it.'

'Come on Local, you can't quit on me now. Not after what we've been through. You're Bonnie to my Clyde. The eggman to my walrus.'

'I can't keep doing this. I need to leave this fucking city tomorrow. And you are going to eventually do something that stops that. So I can't be around you anymore, you're a liability.'

'Suit yourself.'

'This wharf here be OK mate?'

'Perfect. Thank you.'

'Come on Grant, slow down, come back.'
'Forget it. This is the end of this.'
'What about the money?'
'No amount is worth it.'
As if this day could be any worse.

CHAPTER NINE

ONE PM

'Just a Carlton Draught, thanks mate.'

'Ere you go. Seven fifty.'

'Thanks. Sorry it's wet.'

OK, so now what?

You've got seventy five dollars to your name.

No phone.

Your sister's not gonna help you.

At least you've got your beer… on the day you said you'd stop drinking.

How did things get this bad this quickly?

If I'd just minded my business this morning.

Idiot!

Right, well, I guess I need to call Dave and explain this.

He's not gonna be happy.

Call him on what? I don't have his number.

Time check — OH FOR FUCKSAKE!

She still has my watch from the truth or dare game.

The hits just keep on coming.

DAMN!!

Well, I guess I'm off to The Island then.

'Hi.'

'Can I see your invite please?'

'Oh, no I'm here to see someone. Quickly. I'm not staying.'

'You need an invite to come aboard sir.'

'I'm picking up one thing then leaving. I'm with Revolver. Dave Quinn should be here.'

'Wait a minute.'

It's just a floating pontoon you wanker, it's not Fort Knox.

I hate this city.

'OK, Mr Quinn said you're fine.'

'Thanks.'

Twat.

Right, where is she?

The crowd's converged over there so I guess she'll be around there somewhere.

'Excuse me. Pardon me.'

'Thank you guys. So, this next song is called "Temperate Intemperate".

And that's when I saw her, up on stage.

Wow.

She's actually... good.

I don't know what I was expecting, but it's good.

Her voice is... it reminds me of someone...

Who?

Kate Bush?

No...

Feist?

Maybe.

But this song is actually... exquisite.

I would never say that word out loud, but I cannot think of a different way to describe it.

Transcendent, perhaps?

This is not what I expected.

I really like this.

That's my new friend up there.

My cool new friend.

Who I got stoned with.

I got to spend the day with her. How cool is that?

'Thank you.'

WOOOO!

She's great. She's truly truly great.

WOOOOOO!!

'Well well, look what the cat dragged in. I knew you couldn't stay away — you like me too much.'

'Dream on. You still have my watch!'

'Oh yeah, was wondering if you were gonna miss it. I kept that bad boy on the chain around my neck... Oh no...'

'What? Don't tell me you lost it!'

'Oh dear...'

'For fucks —

'— Gotcha. Here you go.'

Thank god.

'So who's "M"?'

'Huh?'

'The engraving on the back of the watch "Never never never give up, M".'

'Mum.'

'Oh. I see.'

'So... that was you up there?'

'That was me.'

'It was good. You know, if you're into that kinda stuff.'

'I'm sure with a large enough shovel I could dig and find a compliment hidden deep down in there, somewhere. Would you like a drink?'

'If you're buying.'

'It's an open bar, but if it breaks your icy demeanour then yes, I'm buying. Beer?'

'Sure, thanks.'

'I'll be right back.'

Hmmm... interesting crowd here, usual Sydney socialite wannabes and beautiful trust fund types.

Music industry wankers and —

'RYDER! Mate, where have you been? It's been ages!'

Oh.

Fuck.

'Oh, hey Andy.'

'Mate! You dropped off the face the Earth? What happened? Where have you been?'

'Ahhh, nowhere man, just, you know, laying low, doing work and that.'

'I heard you moved or were moving overseas.'

'Sorta. Who told you that?'

'Just the word on the streets, heard it around the traps. Mate! It's good to see you. What brings you here?'

'I did.'

Phew, she's back.

'OK very nice. Amazing set up there before

Nina.'

'Thank you.'

'And ahhh, so how do you two—'

'—Me and the Local go WAYYYYY back, don't we?'

'Uh huh.'

'I dig it. Hey, perfect timing, listen, a bunch of us are heading to the grassy knoll for a barbie later, Changa and Squibby and that are gonna be there, they'd love to catch up with you, mate.'

'I don't think I can—'

'—Where is it?'

Stop.

Getting.

Involved!

'The grassy knoll at North Bondi, Grant knows where it is.'

'Yeah, I do and I'd love to, but I don't think I can... cause I've gotta be at this thing soon—'

'—No, you don't.'

'Yes, I really do.'

'No, they called me this morning and said it's been pushed back until tonight. Remember, when you gave them my number cause you lost your phone. I thought I told you that.'

I am going to kill her.

'You lost your phone?'

'Mmmmm. Earlier today.'

'Look it's no big deal mate. I just thought it'd be good to catch up with the boys. It's been so long between drinks.'

'What time is it happening?'

'It kicks off in about an hour.'

'Perfection!'

'Just look for Freddy running around naked, drinking water from a puddle again. So, see you guys out there?'

'You sure will, right Local?'

'Right.'

'OK, cool I gotta go, there's fires to put out backstage. Some drunk idiot's snuck in through the bathroom window and she's started swinging a silver hammer around. Catch you later.'

If I murder her now and dump the body overboard, could I claim temporary insanity?

Stockholm Syndrome?

Happiness would be a warm gun right about now.

'On a scale of one to eleven, how much do you hate me right this minute?'

'I specifically said I didn't want to see anyone I know today. Why did you do that?!'

'We have to go to Bondi anyway.'

'You might have to, I don't. You realise the cops are probably swarming out there looking for us.'

'Rubbish. Those little piggies have better things to do than nab a couple of stoners.'

'We evaded arrest and jumped from a ferry.'

'Pish. Mere details.'

I need the money, I need the money. I need the money.

'So we're going to Bondi. But first, I'm starving. So feed me or so help me, I'll cry instead.'

I need the money, I need the money. I need the money.

'So, you coming or what?'

'Why not? Things can hardly get any worse I suppose.'

'Excellent, cause I haven't finished torturing you yet.'

'The truth is often found in humour.'

'Come on, should we jump in this water taxi?'

'Unless you've got your yellow submarine tied up around here somewhere, it's probably our only way outta here.'

'OK — SHOTGUN!'

I need the money. I need the money. I need the money. I need the money, I need the money. I need the money. I need the money, I need the money. I need the money. I need the money, I need the money. I need the money. I need the money, I need the money. I need the money. I need the money, I need the money. I need the money.

'So Local, what is it you actually do? For work?'

'You half guessed earlier.'

'Cocksucker?'

'Those comedy classes are really paying for themselves today, huh? I worked for the Lonely Planet, writing for their Sydney tour blog.'

'No, but seriously though, what do you — er, did you do?'

'I'm serious.'

'No!'

'Yes.'

'Get the hell outta here! I bet your articles were a barrel of laughs "And if you head here, you'll see... some stupid stuff. And a little further out, some boring old crap."'

'So you *have* read my work?'

'How did you end up in that as a career, given that you hate... well everything?'

'I wasn't always this grizzened. I was backpacking through Europe and doing the rite of passage stint in London, and I just kinda fell into it. Friends of mine were out drinking one night and they met one of the guys who runs the UK office and they told him about this blog that I was keeping on my travels and rah rah rah, four years later here I am still getting paid to tell suckers that The Rocks is a must see.'

'And is it, a must see?'

'I've no idea. I've only ever been once, as a kid. I was on a school excursion when I was about nine. I remember tripping over on a cobbled street, and I cut my knee. I cried like the biggest sook. It was right in front of this girl who I had a huge crush on, Susanna McCartney. She never spoke to me again after that. So I vowed never to return there after that fateful day. And I never have.'

'You let a girl ruin a must-see destination for you?'

'Sometimes a place just holds far too many painful memories.'

'I know you're joking, but still, I've gotta say, you've not put forward a particularly watertight case today as to why this city blows to the level at which you proclaim.'

'Today's been pretty out of the ordinary.'

'You can say that again Local.'

'Today's been pretty out of the ordinary. Shall I say it one more time?'

'Only if you want a kick in the shins.'

'Here's your stop guys, Darling Harbour. That'll

be twenty seven bucks thanks.'
   'It's a bit damp, sorry. Keep the change.'
   'Thanks mate.'
   'After you.'
   'You're so kind. So where are you taking me?'
   'Chinatown?'
   'Perfection!'

CHAPTER TEN

TWO PM

'Have you got the lighter Local?'

'Yeah, I think so. Here it is.'

'Thanks. This place is great. Love the design on the wall inside. I love that old... what do you call it?'

'What?'

'That Asian oriental design look?'

'I don't know. That Asian oriental design look?'

'That's probably it, right. Anyway, I love it. Whenever I see it, it reminds me of this time I was at this Chinese restaurant, in Clapham, and the waiter took my order wrong. He went to the kitchen and a few moments later this duck walked over to our table —'

'— Oh god, not another shit joke —'

'— With a bunch of red roses and whispered in my ear "your eyes sparkle like diamonds". I had to send it back to the kitchen though because I'd ordered the aromatic duck, not a romantic duck.'

'I think you need to sit in the time-out corner.'

'I'm giving you all my best material here, and you're giving me nothing. NOTHING!'

'Do these jokes — and I use the term loosely — work on anyone over the age of three?'

'Your prawn crackers.'

'Thank you.'

'Thanks.'

'Well, you give me your best worst joke then Local.'

'I can't remember any.'

'Sure you can. Everyone can remember one joke.'

'I can't.'

'Try.'

'You're nothing if not persistent. Geez, alright, one joke....'

'Go on.'

'OK, there's one, but it's pretty rotten.'

'The rottener, the better.'

'OK, so an inflatable boy went to—'

'—Inflatable boy?'

'Yeah.'

'OK, go on.'

"So, an inflatable boy went to an inflatable school with inflatable staff and students. One day, he took a pin to school. His principal called him into the office and said, "You've let yourself down, you've let me down, you've let the whole school down".'

"Not bad, not too bad at all. In fact, I may very well pinch that one too.'

'You're welcome to it. So where did this love of dad jokes come from? Or is the answer in the question?'

'No, never really knew my dad. He died when I was very young. No, the appreciation for those came from mum actually. The cheekiest woman I know. She had a lot of things not work out as well as they should, but she always found a way to laugh at life. She's had a tough one though. But yes, my love of the absurd comes from her.'

'You're close?'

'As close as a mum and daughter can be. She's very forgiving. I was a bit of a terror a while back. But she stood by me. What about you?'

'No, I'm not close to my parents.'

'Why not?'

'Just... we're not.'

Change the subject Grant....

'I would have to say the shoes that girl over there is wearing are so exceedingly ugly that they've just shot to the top of my all-time top five worst shoes ever worn by a human being born with the gift of sight.'

'So bad taste in kicks is a deal breaker, huh Local.'

'Huge. I mean really, is it *that* hard to find a decent pair of shoes? There's "wrong", and there's "bad" but they're simply offensive.'

'Why is it such an issue?'

'A woman's taste in footwear says more about them than anything.'

'Jeez. Shallow much? So how are mine?'

'First thing I checked out this morning. Chucks. They're a classic. You pass with flying colours.'

'I'm still trying to work out if you're deliberately trying to wind me up with the rubbish you say or if you genuinely believe this crap.'

'At least, I keep you on your toes.'

'Actually, speaking of shoes, I once bought a pair of sneakers from a drug dealer. I don't know what he laced them with, but I was tripping all day.'

'I'm just gonna let that roll on by.'

'What?! Nothing? Come on. You're a tough crowd.'

'You've got one for every occasion huh?'

'Prepared like a boy scout.'

'Girl scout.'

'Don't be so misogynistic. I can be a boy scout if I want.'

'Suit yourself.'

'So, what are some other deal breakers for you, Local?'

'Hmmm, well if she says she's too busy to read, she may as well say she's too busy to breathe. And lateness. Actually, especially lateness.'

'Fair calls.'

'You see the thing is... I'm not really attracted to women—'

'—You do seem heavily in denial.'

'I don't mean in that way. I mean... I'm not attracted to women in a conventional sense.'

'Explain.'

'I don't understand make-up. Or jewellery or high heels. It's all so unnecessary. Every woman I have ever known, every one I've ever been attracted to, looks their absolute best the moment they get out of the shower. I mean, I understand the ritual of getting dressed up. And the right kind of perfume in small doses has, occasionally, sent me a little bit insane. But if you can find me a woman who isn't at her absolute best with a towel draped around her and water dripping from her skin, then I'll swear off women for life.'

'Interesting.'

'You asked.'

'Well, for me, it's a guy with an awful sense of humour. I mean they must have read these vacuous surveys that say "women prefer a sense of humour over good looks" — which is bullshit, by the way. I'm positive guys concoct those polls. Anyway, they must realise they've a quicker chance toning up their comedy routine than their abs, so they spend the whole time trying to outdo their last rotten attempt at humour, each being slightly less funny than the last.'

'Hold up, you have heard your own jokes, right?'

'Thing is, I can't stand it when a guy is completely unable to inject a bit of wit into a conversation if it goes off the topic of something within their shit little "spontaneous" stand-up schtick. YOU'RE NOT FUNNY! Just fuck off and do some push ups instead.'

'OK, count me off. And one.'

'Get up you idiot.'

'Oww. Fuckity fuck fuck.'

'What?'

'Got a splinter, from the ground. Awwww, the fucker's the size of a gumtree.'

'Oh, come on, give it here. Hmmmm, yeah, I don't know about this, I think we may have to amputate....'

'It's fucking massive.'

'Dream on. And... Three, two, one — it's out.

Crisis avoided, you big baby. You'll be playing the piano again by Tuesday.'

'Is that your professional verdict?'

'I wasn't always a musician. I played a lot of doctors and nurses in my time I'll have you know Local. You'll live.'

'Excuse me, here are your soups.'

'Oh thank you. This looks good.'

'Told you.'

'Hmmm, you're right, this is damned good.'

I think it's time for the old mushroom in the front teeth joke, Grant.

'If you eat all that, you won't have mushroom for anything else.'

'I hate people who play with their food. So childish.'

'I'm really really sorry sir. She's a woman of disrepute. She just learned to walk upright this morning.'

'GET OUT! NOW!'

'I'm so sorry sir. Here's money, to clean. Please take it.'

'Just get out and never come back!'

'Hahahaha, sorry.'

'Did you really have to start a food fight in there?'

'Of course. But you started it.'

'I did not!'

'Did.'

'Is there any chance of you leaving some traces of decency in this city in case I ever feel the need to return?'

'Hmmmmmm...Nah.'

'At least just try to not start a revolution, OK.'

'I'll consider it.'

'You're a living nightmare, you know that, right?'

'Nawww, thank you. You're so sweet. Let's get a drink over there.'

'I'm down. Hopefully they allow children in though.'

'After you, her majesty.'

'Well... I guess it's probably dying without achieving enough. You know, I want to feel like I've accomplished something, that I've created something of worth that lives on when I'm gone. That would be my biggest fear. Not achieving enough.'

'So what's on the list, Local?'

'Of things to accomplish?'

'Yeah.'

'Writing a book is kind of a big one. I'd love to be a published author, traditionally published.'

'An old-fashioned paperback writer huh?'

'Yeah, but I'm realistic that it probably won't ever happen.'

'Why?'

'It's so competitive. And getting more so.'

'Oh, right of course. Sorry, I forgot. Why bother with anything difficult in life.'

'Yeah, yeah I know. Gotta be in it to win it and all that. But I just think that time is running out to do something great with my life.'

'You're still in your thirties. I was once told something that's stuck with me to this day — "It's *never* now or never". And it's true. Time only runs out when you let it run out. You gotta fill it somehow, right?'

'Sure.'

'So what would you write?'

'A novel. I've written about eighty-ish pages of this one idea that I want to finish. One day. I hope to find time for it when I move over to Amsterdam.'

'You're scared of dying with unfulfilled potential — my pet hate in life, by the way — and you've just created the perfect opportunity for yourself to pursue that dream. No distractions, no stupid girls, you're free as a bird. "Life's what happens while you're busy making other plans", no?'

'You're right. I need to do it when I'm there. Definitely.'

'If you only take one thing from today, take that and make sure you follow it.'

'I will.'

'Good.'

'Funnily enough, I kinda wish I also had an ounce of musical talent because I'd like to write music too.'

'Really?'

'Sure. Got nothing standing in my way except for a complete and utter lack of melodious virtuosity.'

'Hmmmm. Sit tight.'

'Where are you going?'

'To the bar; don't go anywhere.'

'OK.'

'Excuse me.'

'Yes, what can I get for you?'

'Do you have a couple of pieces of paper behind the bar that I could steal?'

'Ahhh, let's see... yep, here you go.'

'Thank you so much. Actually, I'll grab a couple more of those beers while I'm here. What were they again?'

'Young Henry's Newtowner?'

'Perfect, two more of those thanks.'

'OK, I'll bring them out.'

'Thank you so much. Ooooh, actually, can I borrow that pen?'

'Go ahead.'

'You're a dream, thanks.'

Dooooo doooo deee dahhhh doo da deeeeee.

'I'm back.'

'So I can see. What's the paper for?'

'We're about to tick something off that list of yours.'

'What do you mean?'

'Patience is a virtue my young friend. So sit there a moment and be virtuous.'

'Here's your beers, guys.'

'Thanks.'

'Thank you so much.'

And now I'll just fold this piece of paper over a little at the top so he can't see what I wrote.

'OK, I've written the first line of a song, but you can't read it until then end. Now it's your turn, you write the next line.'

'But how will I know what the rhythm is? Or what the song's about?'

'Just create your own rhythm. Then you follow yours and I'll follow mine.'

'Hmmmm, OK. This could fun. Let's see....'

Look at him scrunching up his cute little face, wracking his brain.

'Nope... I'm drawing a blank. What should I write about?'

'It's your song.'

'Well, what do you usually write about?'

'Anything.'

'Can you be a little less vague?'

'OK, write about home... or heartbreak... or civil unrest in Uganda.'

'Argh, it's too much pressure! I'm coming up with nothing.'

'OK fine, I'll give you start. Write about... today. Write about what happened today *but...* write it as if it's from the point of view of a toy.'

'A toy? What kind of toy?'

'I'm not doing all the work for you! Think for yourself.'

'OK, a toy... living what I've experienced today... OK.'

There he goes... writing away there.

If he wasn't such a miserable twat, he'd actually be kinda cute.

What am I doing?!

Monkey swinging already?!

You only just broke up with someone twelve hours ago, you twit.

'Here you go.'

'No, fold it over first so I can't see.'

'Oh, OK. Your turn.'

'OK... let's see... Ah, yes, I've got my next line.'

Dooo deeee deee dash dash dooo dee dee.

'And back to you sir. No peeking!'

'I wasn't.'

'Can we smoke here?'

'Think so. Yeah, there's an ashtray.'

'Want one?'

'I'm good thanks.... I read this thing once that Paul McCartney — you heard of him?'

'Really tall guy, sells apples down the market, wears an eye patch.'

'That's him. Well anyway, he woke from a dream one night with the fully formed melody and lyrics to "*Yesterday*" in his head. And he frantically jotted it down before it passed back into the night. Here you go, your turn.'

'Thanks.'

'But as it was so simple, he worried that he'd caught a case of cryptomnesia and had subconsciously plagiarised the tune from something he'd previously heard, so initially, he considered that it would be best to not play it to anyone and just bin it.'

'Seriously?'

'That's what I read. You done?'

'Yep.'

'My turn.'

'Well Local, I'd say John and Paul have got nothing on us.'

'Damn right. So what about you?'

'Huh?'

'Greatest fear?'

'Spiders.'

'Standard.'

'And spending my life with the wrong person.'

CHAPTER ELEVEN

THREE PM

Time check — 3.13.

So five hours til her sound check.

OK, after a bumpy morning we are back on track, and all is going fine. Maybe this will all work out in the wash. I should end up with a bit of extra cash in hand actually when it's all said and done. Winning all around.

Plus... I guess I'm having fun with her. She's a tornado of destruction but... the funnest kind.

'OK Local, your turn to shine. I want to see your writing skills.'

'How?'

'Describe me.'

'What? I haven't got any paper.'

'No, just describe me verbally. Just like you were introducing a character in your book.'

'You're serious?'

'Completely. OK, I'll start you off... "She strolled into his life like a dot dot dot."'

'I... no, I... I'm not in the mood. It's too hot for

this. Can't you just appreciate the tourist trap that you demanded I bring you to and enjoy the view?'

'OK, Sydney Opera House. Amazing. Ticked that box, done. Now describe me.'

'No.'

'Come on.'

And the tornado of destruction begins again.

'NO!'

'God, you can be annoying Local. Sheesh. Alright, we'll I'm gonna take a seat.'

'On the steps, right in the middle of the thoroughfare. Real smart.'

'If you're not gonna entertain me, I have to entertain myself.'

'Fine. Let's sit.'

'Now... where is it?'

'What are you looking for?'

'Ahh here it is?'

'A portable speaker?'

'Precisely. Switch that on. And now a quick scan through Spotify... and bingo! La laaa ahh nah lahhla.'

'You're not playing.... YOU ARE! Stop it! Turn it off now!'

'But you're such a huge fan.'

'I mean it, give it here.'

'You ready, here's the chorus, all together now — "IF I COULD TURN BACK TIME!"'

'People are looking.'

'Let 'em — "I'D GIVE IT ALL FOR YOU".'

'You're getting the words wrong.'

'Ha! I knew you were a fan —"AND MAYBE BABY YOU'D STAY".'

'Turn it off. Please!'

'No. Dance with me.'

'No!'

'Dance with me for one verse and I will.'

'FINE! One verse, that's all.'

OK Grant, block out the world, it's fine. No one here knows you, you don't know them. You're simply dancing on the steps of the Sydney Opera House, with a deranged woman, to Cher.

'"I DIDN'T REALLY MEAN TO HURT YOU".'

'"I DIDN'T WANT TO SEE YOU GO!"'

'I knew you loved it.'

'"AND YOU'D LOVE ME LOVE ME LOVE ME LIKE YOU USED TO DO". And spin!'

'WHOO!'

I should not be enjoying this as much as I am.

'And another spin.'

'Whoa!'

'Whoops, was almost a spin to forget. Here comes the solo.'

'You've got moves Local, I'm impressed.'

'Wasn't just a distrust of religion and the physics behind the perfect paper plane I picked up in Catholic school. And... Spin!'

'Ahhh, whoa... Quick Local, catch meEEEEE!'

'Look out!'

'OWWWWW!'

'Oh. Shit... are you, are you OK?'

That's not good... that was a break.

'My hand... I landed on my hand and it bent back.'

That was definitely a break I heard.

Shit.

'Paging Doctor Robert, paging Doctor Robert to ward 3.'

'Well, the good news is that it's not a break, but your wrist should be rested for the next few days. A week ideally.'

'A week? Really? So, I shouldn't use it at all?'

'Not unless you plan on drawing out the recovery. You can take these for any pain.'

'OK, thank you doctor.'

'They said if I fell differently, I would have broken it but it's just sprained. But it means I can't perform tonight.'

'I'm so so sorry, I'm such a dick.'

'It was an accident. And given that you'd be on a plane somewhere over Asia right now if you'd never met me, let's just notch it up as one each for karma.'

'It's nice of you to say, but I still feel responsible.'

'Oh you are. I just don't think there's any point dwelling on it. Right. Well, I've tried to call Dave a few times and he's not answering plus I tried the label, but there's no one there on Saturday. I don't know who else to try?'

'So, you really think you'll have to cancel the show?'

'I don't think I have a choice. Unless you have a

set of mad guitar skills you've surreptitiously been holding out on me?'

'If I could, I would. How long would it take for me to learn the fine art of the guitar then master all your songs?'

'About six hours, but we only have four.'

'Damn.'

'You don't know anyone who might be able to help?'

'Teach me advanced guitar playing in four hours?'

'No, who is a musician who could step in and play with me.'

'Oh.... No.... Well. No, not really.'

'There's a wavering hint of doubt in there.'

'I used to know someone. Once. Amazing guitarist. Session musician mainly.'

'Can you contact him or her?'

'Yeah, we're not really on speaking terms. I doubt he'll want to be doing me any favours.'

'Could you at least try? Please? Time heals all wounds, doesn't it?'

'Not sure that much time has past.'

'Give it a go? For me?'

I guess I'm contacting him.

This won't go well.

'Sure. Lend me your phone and I'll call someone.'

'Here.'

'Just gotta look up the number.'

Please please please me rock gods and come through on this, and let Marco overlook the past so he'll help Nina out.... please!

If you do, I promise I'll go to church every

weekend for the rest of my life.

And twice during Lent.

'Prudence, hi it's Grant. Grant Ryder. Yeah, it's been a while. I'm actually looking to track down Marco. Do you know where I might find him today? Yeah, I know, but I want to try and talk with him anyway. So he's at The Domain, at the amphitheatre doing a tech rehearsal. OK, thanks. I will. Thanks.'

'So?'

'He should be at the Domain in the city. I'll warn you though, I wouldn't expect much.'

'We can only try, right?'

'That we can.'

Hmmm, well this should at least ensure the day stays on course to be the worst ever.

Well... second worst.

CHAPTER TWELVE

FOUR PM

'Check one, check one two. Testing, testing. You getting that?'

'OK, got it, thanks Marco.'

'And are you getting a line on this centre guitar?'

'Yeah, all good. It's coming through perfect.'

'Great.'

'Ummm, hi Marco. How have you been?'

Annnnnnd that's actually a slightly lesser stare of evil than I was expecting. Only two daggers shot in my direction, not the whole kitchen drawer this time.

'The fuck are you doing here Ryder?'

'It's been a while.'

'Not long enough in my books.'

'Have you been well?'

'What do you want?'

'I... ummm, we bought you this.'

'Bottle of vodka. What have I done to deserve that?'

'It's just a... gift.'

'You'd do better with it. I'm surprised it's not half empty already.'

He's at least thawed slightly since the last time.

Not.

'This is Nina. Taylor.'

'I know who you are.'

Am I the only person on Earth who doesn't know her?

'She's performing tonight, but she's had a little incident and we need to find a replacement guitarist.'

'I injured my wrist earlier. Fell on it awkwardly.'

'Bummer for you.'

'Look Marco, I know the last thing I could expect is for you to do something for me. But as a professional favour, to Nina, could you maybe help her out?'

'He said you were the only person in Sydney worth asking.'

'Did he now?'

'Absolutely. And if I don't find a guitarist to fill in, I'll have to cancel my show. I can pay you of course. Whatever you need, as well.'

'Listen, I'm not interested, OK. Your friend here can explain why.'

'Marco, can you just put the past aside for one night to help her out? Please?'

'So you can be a knight in shining armour for the latest damsel in distress? Pass.'

'Please Marco, I'm desperate.'

'Look, I'm sorry about your gig, and your wrist. But you're wasting your time. I've gotta get back to work.'

'Marco... I'm sorry, OK.'

'Excuse me? I missed that. What did you say?'

'I'm sorry for what I did. I was in a fucked up place. It was dumb.'

'Wow. OK, you know what... you've won me over. I'll do it.'

'Really?'

'NO!'

And off he goes.

'Told you not to expect much. Let's go and see if there's someone else we can speak to.'

'Local.... I don't know what you did or what's happened in the past; it's none of my business. But whatever it is, obviously hurt him. I'm not saying this for the sake of the gig... but it seems like you need to apologise to him for whatever happened.'

'I just did.'

'Do it properly. Say what you need to say. Make amends.'

She's right. If I leave tomorrow and never see him again.... I need to make this right.

Or at least show him that I fucking hate myself for what happened.

Deep breath.

One.

Two.

Three.

'Grant has something to say. I'll just go and wait over at the mixing desk.'

'Ryder, can't you just leave? Seriously?'

'Just let me say this.'

'Fine! But you have one minute, then I call security.'

'OK. Marco, I'm very... very sorry for what I did.'

'You can do better than that. Forty-five seconds.'

'I... I don't know what you want me to say. I mean, I still can't really remember doing it. But I'm truly sorry for what I'm told I did.'

'You stole my car.'

'I didn't steal it.'

'You didn't *ask* to drive my car, so you stole it. Because you needed to know where she was and what she was doing. I get it, OK, I get how much she meant, but she moved on, and you couldn't let it go. And nothing any of us said would get through to help you. Do you know how useless that made us feel, watching you go down this long and winding road of self-destruction? Christ knows how you didn't kill anyone that night, you arrogant prick, but not once have you even offered to pay after you totalled it. After what you had *just* experienced... it should have been a wake-up call against pulling shit like that. But the rules apply to everyone but you, don't they?'

'I'm sorry. I am. I was messed up.'

'I'm sick of hearing that. We're all sick of it. You hide behind that every time, saying "my life's fucked and so I need a drink" and just go around in self-destruct mode. And it breaks our fucking hearts. We were there for you. Taking the phone calls at all hours. Listening to you pour your heart out. And you repay us by... treating us like trash. It's not on. It's not.'

'I've been trying to get my shit together. I know I keep fucking up. Because I fucking hate myself. Hate what I've caused. And I can't make a change in this city. I'm just going around in circles, doing the same fucking thing every week... every weekend. Making everything worse. That's why I'm leaving.'

'Where are you going?'

'Amsterdam.'

'That place should really set you on the straight and narrow.'

'Maybe, maybe not, but I don't have any other option. I need to find a place where I know things are getting better. I was meant to leave this morning. But I even fucked that up. Look, I hate that I've caused this. That I've driven all you guys away. The only family I've got is a sister who can barely look at me. I haven't heard from my dad in a year. I'm so fucking alone here. I just need to get somewhere that I won't feel judged for being such a screw up. Amsterdam is all I can think to do.'

'Have you been seeing anyone? A counsellor?'

'Yeah, been through a bunch of 'em. They all want me on meds.'

'Maybe you should. They generally know best. It's what they're paid for, y'know.'

'I don't want to get into a conversation about that now.... Look, I'm sorry to just turn up here. I knew it would not go well. How could it? Cause you have every right to feel this way. Every right. I'm just so... sincerely sorry. If I could take it all back.... If there was some way I could change it, I would. And I'm sorry it's taken so long to apologise... I've just been so completely ashamed and embarrassed to face you about it. I'm sorry for turning up. I'm... I'm leaving.'

'Grant.'

'Yeah?'

'...You were always a better person off the drink.

One of the best. I just wish you could see it.'
'I know.... I know.'

'How did it go?'
'Come on, let's go.'
'Oh.'
'Ryder, wait.'
'Marco?'
'So.... I hope I don't regret asking this but... what time's the gig?'
'Ten.'
'OK, well if —IF— I help, you're not off the hook. You have a long, long LOOOOOOONG way to go to make up for this Grant. Not just to me, but to Sally. And everyone.'
'Whatever it takes, I will make it right.'
'Yes, you will.'
'So you'll help her? You'll fill in on guitar?'
'I've got bills to pay, and she needs a band so let's quit wasting time yappin' and get to work. The clock's ticking.'
'Seriously?'
'Thank you Marco.'
'Yeah yeah, OK enough with the hugs. Nina, let's head to the breakout area in the back, should be quiet enough. Ryder, you should go chill somewhere.'
'OK. Nina, you all good?'
'Go. Go and chill for a while.'
'OK, I'll be back in an hour or so.'
'Enjoy.'
Wow. So that just happened. I guess I underestimated what an amazing person Marco is.

CHAPTER THIRTEEN

FIVE PM

I've gotta make this change count.

For real, not just because it's what they want.

It's got to be for good. These can't be empty words backed up without action.

Otherwise, I'll just fall straight back into what I was doing, just in a different time zone.

I am good...

I do have value...

I'm not completely worthless.

But I keep fucking up.

I can change. I just need to stay focussed.

And believe in myself.

I can do this.

No more drinking.

I'm done.

Done.

DONE!

It's time to grow up.

I owe it to my friends.

Owe it to myself primarily though.

Speaking of which... time check — 5.37.
I'd better go find Nina.

'So I'll contact the guys now and tell them about what's happened, put your name on the list and I'll see you there at seven thirtyish, OK Marco?'

'The Spiegeltent at half seven. Done. And I meant what I was saying Nina, I really, really like your stuff. It's simple yet beautiful.'

'Beautifully simple, probably a good thing given the bind I'm in, which you've heroically have saved me from. Come here, I need to hug you once more time.'

'Ahhh, leave me some air to breathe.'

'I can't, I just want to thank you so much.'

'Yes, sincerely Marco, thank you Marco. For helping... for everything.'

'It's OK Ryder.'

'We good?'

'We're good. OK, I gotta get back to prepping here so I can hand it over, so I'll see you later.'

'Thanks Marco.'

'See you guys.'

'This is amazing! I have a guitarist! Marco is definitely one of the good guys.'

'Yeah. Yeah he is.'

'So I was thinking Local... what do you say we head out to Bondi now, drop into that grassy knoll shindig?'

'Yeah nah, I think that was more than an adequate humility trip for one day. I can do without going out and being the fool on the hill.'

'Do you feel like talking about what happened? With Marco and these friends you're avoiding?'

'Life just not going to plan... A handful of disgraceful moments that would not make a mother proud, being the end result of a regular breakfast of cheap vodka and self-pity. I just kinda lost it. My grip on things. On everything. I'd get fucked up every night, turn up at parties, invited or otherwise and act like a fool, get thrown out, pass out, usually in a rose bush — fall asleep, wake up, repeat.... And the whole time I could see what I was doing, but... it just felt like it was happening to someone else — I'm not saying that as an excuse... it just didn't feel like it was me doing it...'

'Dignity can be overrated when you have a broken heart.'

'That was part of it, I guess.'

'So they abandoned you? Your friends?'

'No, it was more so that I kept my distance from them, out of shame. I got the feeling they were sick of dealing with my crap and what I was bringing to their lives. There were times I just went too far.'

'Everyone's got at least one love who drove 'em to do crazy shit. Thing that sucks is more often than not, the ones that we lose it over are never the ones that actually deserve that level of misappropriated sociopathic devotion... it's never the ones that actually treat us well.'

'Hmmm.'

'Look, we don't have to go out to Bondi. But, you know, you're on a plane to a new life in the morning.... And after tomorrow, you'll probably never see them again.'

'Wouldn't you rather continue your crime

spree?'

'There's plenty of time for that later. Come on, let's grab a cab. I'm paying. Besides, I need to get out there anyway.'

'Oh yeah, your secret mission. Want to elude what that all about?'

'You'll see.'

'Alright, let's head out there. But if I say we have to leave, we leave. Cool?'

'Deal. There's one — TAXI!''

Sitting in the back of a cab on the way to what could be the most humiliating moment of my life.

Just get it over and done with, I suppose.

What's the worst that can happen?

They tell you to leave.

At least my fears will have been justified, I guess.

It's true though, after tomorrow I don't ever have to see these people ever again.

Or this city.

It's funny, this time yesterday I never thought I'd miss a single thing about this damn place.

Now… I'm not so certain.

This *is* my home.

Well… as close to a home as you can have when you don't feel connected to anywhere.

And I haven't for a long, long time now.

'Can I ask you a question?'

'I think we're past asking if we can ask each other questions now Local. So shoot.'

'What does "home" mean to you? The word, the

idea of "home".'

'Where I feel most comfortable.'

'Which is?'

'These days… I think the second whatever plane I'm on leaves the ground, to the moment the wheels touch down again. Strange I guess, cause I feel more at ease up there, not tied to any one place. There's nowhere else I can be and no one expecting anything from me. So bizarrely, that's what home is for me, right in this moment of my life... where I feel most at ease...'

'Is London not home?'

'It's *a* home. And I think eventually I want to lay my roots there again… or close enough to it. But I've put a lot of things on hold to do this, to chase my dream — friends, relationships, birthdays, weddings, births, dental appointments. I can't remember the last birthday I spent with my close friends. Even financial security — at any moment now, this could all fall apart.'

'Does that scare you?'

'Not really. It should. Cause I have no idea what else I'd be doing right now. But I grew up having just enough to get by — mum was not really well off, and any money we had went on rent or medicine. So, I learnt early on how to make the most of what was on offer. Easy come, easy go was a motto I've lived by for a long time, but it always finds a way to even out.'

'My dad used to drill financial responsibility in us from like when we were three.'

'And I'll bet it made you completely irresponsible for a while.'

'Oh god, absolutely.'

'Haha. So how much further it is?'

'We're just at the top of Bondi Junction so about three minutes.'

'Good, cause I'm SOOOOOO hungry.'

'You just ate.'

'No I didn't.'

'Well, we *almost* just ate before you decided to call "food fight".'

'I'm always hungry. Come on, indulge me. I hope there's food there.'

'It's called a barbecue for a reason. They used to put pretty huge spreads on so I can't imagine this one won't be any different. There's generally at least a pig on a spit.'

'That should do for starters, I guess.'

'I'll phone ahead and make sure they have one set up just for you.'

'Yum!'

'Ahhh, you can just drop us here thanks mate.'

'OK...Twenty five dollars and forty cents.'

'Here you go sir and keep the change.'

'Thanks, and have a good afternoon.'

OK Grant, breathe, smile, be open.

You can do this.

My god, my heart is racing so fast...

Can I do this?

What am I doing?

'I... I ahhh...'

'Shhhh.'

And that's when she just took my hand.

And it feels... nice.

...It feels nice.

And almost in an instant, my heart slows down.

Nawww... he looks so awkward. Just walking to see his friends.

I feel sorry for him, the level of self-hatred he must have to feel this anxious just seeing his friends.

What goes on in that mind of his?

I'd best just keep an eye on him, and pull him away if it all goes wrong...

'Hey Local, what did the cow say to the farmer?'

'What?'

'When are you gonna stop playing with my tits and just fuck me?'

Finally, a laugh!

CHAPTER FOURTEEN

SIX PM

'Oh my god — Grant! Babe! Look who's here guys!'

'Hi Julia, hey Jude. Baxy.'

'Grant! Ohhhh mate! Where have you been?'

'So good to see you.'

'Hi guys. Everyone this is —'

'—OH MY GOD, is that... it is! It's Nina Taylor!'

'Hi, hi, hi there. Nice to meet you.'

'Oh wow! Grant, you're full of surprises.'

'She's a friend.'

'Your music is so *so* beautiful.'

'Really. Best road trip album ever. Bar none!'

'Oh, thank you. That's really kind. Oooh, I love your brooch. What is it?'

'It's a blackbird.'

'It's so cute.'

'Thank you, my boyfriend just bought it for me. You have to come and meet him, he'll flip!'

'OK?'

'You alright with this?'

'It's what I deal with every day Local. But are you OK?'

'Yeah... yeah I think things are OK.'

'Well, go and mingle with them.'

'You sure? You don't need me to help. They can get a bit...umm, possessive.'

'I can handle myself.'

But I like that he cares...

And this goes well.

I can see the inner light coming back on within him, as he realises that his friends love him.

He sees that he can be happy again.

And after a while of talking with his admittedly lovely friends, I can sense, from the look he gives me across the group, that he wants what I want.

To have it just be "our time" again.

'Excuse me girls, can I just borrow Nina for a moment?'

'Never, she's ours and we're not letting her go.'

'Errr OK, seems like I've been adopted by your friends Local.'

'Yes, she ours and we're gonna feed her and house her and —'

'—OK before this becomes even weirder than it is, we have to make a move.'

'Yes, sorry girls. I don't want to spoil the party, but I have a show tonight, gotta start heading in and getting ready.'

And then he takes my hand. It's clammy... but still, it feels strong, as he holds tight and I feel like he never wants to let go.

'Alright, I'll catch up with you guys another time.'

'SOOOOO lovely to meet you all.'

'You too Nina!'

'You're as sweet as I always thought you'd be.'

'Thank you.'

'See you guys.'

'BYE!'

And we walk away from his circle of friends, his hand clutching mine. Like it's the most natural thing in the world.

My god, am I... falling for him?!

I'd be lying if I didn't say...

...a little... maybe.

'So the question you wanted to know before... about "why today?"'

'Yes.'

'Do you still want to know the reason?'

'Absolutely.'

'OK... It's not far from here.'

'Here we are.'

'Wow!'

'This was mum's favourite place in the world.'

'It's beautiful. Is that lighthouse still functioning?'

'Sure is. Called Hornby's Lighthouse. It's almost 150 years old. Ships come in around the heads, just through there. It's the most eastern tip of Sydney.'

'It's really stunning.'

'Mum grew up not far from here, about fifteen minutes' walk. When we were young, like really little, she'd bring us here all the time. She'd tell us that over there behind that cliff was where rainbows started. She was full of wild stories. When she was in her twenties, she was living in London and she followed the Rolling Stones around on tour for four months, through Europe and then eventually they let her hang with them on tour in the States for a while.'

'No way!'

'She knew them all, the Stones, Zeppelin. She even met John Lennon a couple of times. Said she almost ended up running away with a tour manager from the States, so I should count my lucky stars dad came along.'

'Did they meet in London, your parents?'

'No, in Melbourne. In a record store of all places. She was back briefly for a friend's wedding, he was in town for business — both were only there for a few days. Anyway, they ended up having an argument in the store — Stones versus Beatles — mum said the Stones obviously, but dad was adamant it was the Beatles who were the finer band. It got pretty heated, from how they described it, so much so that mum ripped up a copy of "Sgt Pepper's" in front of him. Got them both chucked out. And then something clicked from that meeting. Dad said it was how passionately she argued with him, even though he swears he was right and she was wrong. So, they went for a coffee, talked more, for ages actually. Then they exchanged details, and mum went back to her exciting London life, and dad back here to his job with the taxman. But neither one could stop thinking about that moment in the music store. So they started to write to each other, over a year or so — exchanging bands they should check out, mailing LPs back and forth and what not. Eventually, mum realised that she'd fallen in love, so she had to come home to be with him.'

'Wow.'

'And on their first date, they came here. As a laugh, dad bought her a copy of "Sgt. Pepper's" and when he gave it to her, she launched it right over the edge... and the rest, as they say, is history.'

'It's such a great story.'

'Yeah. I've always liked knowing I was here because of the Beatles.'

'I've always thought a record store is the most romantic place in the world. Being surrounded by all those tiny little snapshots of hearts broken and mended again through song.'

'It really sucks that they're disappearing. That the concept of a physical place you go to get music is becoming a distant memory. Kids grow up thinking that music is something that they deserve to get for free, when it's one of the most valuable things in the world.'

...And, as I realise I've danced around the subject enough, it's time to open the flood gates and tell her all.

'It was a year ago today that... she died.'

'Oh. I see.'

'Two days before that, Abigail broke up with me. I took it really terribly. Like a spoilt brat actually. Turned straight to drinking... drugs. Whatever would make me feel something else... Anyway, I was drunk out of my head, almost to the point of blacking out on that night and... I went around to her house, trying to beg her to reconsider. But I ended up being a dick, so she called the cops. They came... took me away. Put me in a holding cell to sober up. I called mum to come and collect me... And on her way... some guy ran a red light. He ran a red light... It was an accident. A stupid, piss poorly-timed accident that could have happened at any time. But it didn't. It happened at that time.'

'And it was a year ago?'

'To the day.... I guess now you can see why I didn't want to be here today.'

'And what about your dad?'

'He took it about as well as I did. He shut down. Threw himself into work. Didn't go catatonic, but might as well have.'

'When did you last see him?'

'The day of the funeral. We came down here, scattered her ashes. Then he carved this into the railing.'

'All my loving, my dear Martha Ryder, November 10, 1951 – January 5, 2016.... she was sixty four.'

'That was the last thing I saw him do.'

'That's so sad. I'm really sorry.'

'Thanks... but what can you do you know... what can you do?'

'What's that over there, leaning against that post? Do you see it? I'll go get it'

'What is it?'

'Wow... It's... a copy of "Sgt. Pepper's", on vinyl.'

'Show me.'

I don't believe it....

'He... he must have been here.'

'Is that surprising?'

'The last I heard he was living in New York, but could be anywhere really.'

'Maybe it's time to track him down again?'

'No. If he wants to be found, he will.'

'Maybe this was his way of saying he wants to be found?'

'Maybe...'

Fuck him though.

'I think we should start heading off. We don't want to miss the soundcheck.'

'Are you OK?'

'Yeah, yeah I'm fine... but let's get out of here, OK?'

'OK.'

...goodbye mum. I'm sorry I let you down, again.

'Well, if the map isn't lying... I think it should just down here. Ah-ha, lovely! And this is it!'

'I've got a feeling I'm not going to like this. Are you going to tell me what you're doing or should I wait until the arraignment to find out?'

'Probably the less you know, the better. All I need you to do is be the lookout while I drop one thing off and pick up another.'

'Whoa, OK, time out. I'm not getting involved with drugs. You're on your own.'

'Local, come back. Come back here. It's not drugs OK. Neither is it strictly legal. It's not really illegal. I don't think. It's just... a bit naughty. Here, look at this.'

'Your water-logged itinerary. So?'

'Look on the back.'

'Right...?'

'OK, so there's this game I play, with my grandfather, and every city either of us visit, we liberate one specific item *but* replace it with an exact same one from the last city you were in.'

'OK?'

'When he was in the war, his platoon used to do it all the time.'

'Which war?'

'Korean. Whoever managed to liberate the particular thing from a city— would you be a dear and get me that bin over there— and then replace it with a similar one, one from another place, and not get caught, won the money they'd pooled.'

'And you play this with your pop?'

'Uh huh. He told me about it when I was young, and I always liked the idea of it, so I just... re-appropriated it. I love that old buggar. Has a joke for every occasion, just like mum.'

'So... what's this thing you're liberating?'

'It's in my bag. Hold this.'

'A screwdriver? You've liberated a screwdriver? Very novel.'

'No silly, It's not that. I need the screwdriver to help remove what the thing is.'

'And are you going to tell me what it is or just keep me in suspense?'

'Here, *this* is the mission.'

'You're joking?!'

'I never joke about this.'

'And you've been carrying a street sign around all day.'

'Yes and I'm going to take down the one over on that wall and put this one up in its place. And while I do that, you're gonna keep watch and take photos as proof.'

'Evidence more like.'

'It's not illegal.'

'I'm pretty certain it would be.'

'Here, just take the camera, I've got work to do.'

'Well, you've certainly got a knack for petty crime.'

'Merci beaucoup. And… there's the second screw out. Now take this one and hand me that other one.'

'Swapping street signs across the globe huh?'

'It just my little way of leaving my mark on each city I visit. You still keeping watch?'

'Yeah yeah, it's all clear.'

'And.... Voila!'

'Nice job, little crooked but the job's done.'

'So does that answer your question from earlier about the Beatles?'

'Perfectly.'

'Come and stand in front of it with me.'

'No, I have a no selfies policy.'

'You want a kick in the shins again?'

'Fine.'

'OK. And on the count of three say "crafty

misdemeanour"!'

SNAP.

'There, now it's captured for all posterity.'

'Great, proof I was at the scene of yet another crime. What's your tally from today at now anyway?'

'Let's see... there's the vodka at the airport, so theft, but I did kinda pay for it.'

'So pillaging.'

'Yep. Then smoking weed in public, evading arrest, jumping from a moving ship, starting a food fight, though I'm not sure that's technically a crime. We didn't pay for the bus ride there and now this. So, what six?'

'What's your record?'

'I think it was about twelve in one day once a few years back. Not that I'm keeping tally.'

'Course not. Anyway, we should head back to the city. It'll start getting busy there soon —'

'—Oi, you two, I saw what you were doing on the CCTV. Stay where you are!'

'Shit, run!!!!'

'Fuck!'

'Is this crime number seven?'

Annnnnnd, we're off and running... Again.

'Nice...work...eagle-eye... Remind me... to never ask... you to... be look out... in a jailbreak.'

'Given your penchant... for petty crime... I don't imagine that day's... far away.'

'I'm puffed...'

'We're both... so out of... shape.'

'Speak for your... self.'

'Whatever Usain.'

'Is this our bus coming?'

'Nope, we need the one after the 909. Here's the one we want, the 380.'

'This goes all the way to the city?'

'Yeah. I'll pay... just grab that seat.'

'Done.'

'Sit there and try not to vandalise the seat. Or blow up the bus.'

'I don't think you're meant to say things like "blow up the B.U.S." when you're on a B.U.S. Local'

'Two day tripper ticket please.'

'Here ya go.'

'Thanks.'

This is the most fun non-date I've ever had.

In fact, this is the most fun I've ever had with another person.

She's extraordinary.

Nothing affects her, nothing bothers her.

I love that about her.

'Hmmm hmmmmm doo hmmm doo dooo deee.'

'What's that you've got?'

'It's the lyrics we wrote earlier.'

'Oh yeah, I completely forgot about that — gimme a look.'

'No!'

'Oh, go on!'

'Later, you'll have to wait.'

'You've been saying that all day. Ugh, if this kid doesn't stop kicking the back of my seat, he's not gonna live to see his next birthday.'

'Just settle down Local. He's not hurting you.'

Ugh.

Ugh.

Once more and he's had it.

Ugh.

Right.

'Hey kiddo, I know given that you're dressed up in your Iron Man costume you think you're invincible, but can you stop kicking my seat please?'

'Jeffery, stop kicking his seat. I'm sorry.'

'It's OK.'

'See, you handle things nicely and they get sorted.'

'You're right. I may have just formed a new habit—'

Ugh.

Ugh.

Stop kicking kid...

Ugh.

I'm serious…

Ugh.

'Local... behave yourself.'

Once more.

Just once more…

I DARE YOU…

Ugh.

'Local!'

'Look you little brat. I asked you nicely. If you keep it up, I'll tell you the truth about Santa. And the Easter Bunny. And you're not gonna like it!'

'Kicked off a bus for starting a fight with a toddler.

That's gotta be a first?'

'YEAH! YEAH! I'LL TAKE YA! AND DC IS WAY BETTER THAN MARVEL ANYWAY, YOU LITTLE RAT!'

'You got that out of your system now?'

'What was I supposed to do? He was kicking my seat!'

'Ummm, you could have let it go.'

'I was in the right.'

'He's three years old.'

'Whatever. We can walk from here anyway.'

'Fine.'

'Are you mad at me?'

'No. I just think it's interesting that that's how you handled that situation.'

'I'm no angel.'

'You don't say.'

'…sorry. You're right, I should have been more diplomatic.'

'It's fine. To be completely honest… If you didn't do something, I was going to anyway.'

'He was a little shit, right?'

'Oh, the worst.'

'Thank you!'

'You still shouldn't have done it.'

'We'll agree to disagree. Made me ponder something though.'

'What's that?'

'At what age does it become socially unacceptable to wander through the city dressed in a superhero costume anyway?'

'Ummm, I think "never".'

'You know, for once, I think you might be right.'

CHAPTER FIFTEEN

SEVEN PM

'Well if I do say so myself, I think between us we picked up some pretty nifty costumes from that thrift store.'

'I heartily agree Local, or should I say Karateman slash Wonder Boy slash Commando General.'

'So Thrift Store Wonder Woman slash Robin slash Someone with a lightning bolt across their neither-bits, how are you feeling about your gig?'

'Well, when life gives you lemons, or closer to the point, when life gives you a sprained wrist.'

'I meant moreso with your break up. How are you feeling about that?'

'Yeah… I was thinking I'll pull a couple of songs from the set. Not really feeling up to singing them tonight, given the memories they're laced with. But life goes on, you know. If I dropped songs from my set cause of a bad experience after the fact, my show would consist of me walking on stage, saying "Thank you and Goodnight" and doing a runner before the crowd started hurling tomatoes.'

'I guess it must come as par for the course.'

'You learn to work with it. So, what are we doing now, just wandering aimlessly?'

'Not aimlessly so much, just people watching Sydneysiders. There's usually some cool attractions and exhibits down alleys if you're adventurous enough to seek them out on opening night of the festival.'

'OK. Uh-ohhhh, look out — small child approaching us, one o'clock. Should I restrain you? Do you feel the need to lash out at another one?'

'I'm not that curmudgeonly.'

'You are.'

'He looks happy though, right? Doesn't that kid looks happy?'

'I guess. No more or less than anyone else his age without a care greater than "Where did I leave my Incredible Hulk pencil case?"'

'D'you ever look at a little kid smiling or laughing at something and wonder like, "how do we ever know what is actually funny?". Do you know what I mean?'

'Kind of?'

'Like... how do we get our sense of humour? Where does it come from? You can't teach it. Everything else we learn as kids has a logic — maths, grammar, building things and all that stuff, it all has a reasoning behind it — but where does an understanding of and appreciation of humour come from?'

'Dick and fart jokes I guess.'

'Ha... that may not be completely far from the

truth.'

Was that... is she crying? She is.

'Are you OK?'

'It's nothing.'

'Did I say something?'

'No, no, nothing like that.'

'Stop. What is it?'

'It's nothing.'

'It's something.... I'm sorry I shouldn't have brought up your ex.'

Idiot!

'It's not that. It's... just... well today. All of a sudden. Right now, I just feel really really... homesick.'

'Oh.'

'I worked out earlier this morning that I've been on the road, away from home now for almost four months. Working, meeting new people through work and... I don't get many genuine experiences lately. People are usually saying how much this or that song means to them — which is great, but sometimes I just feel like a collage of these impressions people project onto me cause of what they take from my music. Constantly being "on" eight days a week, it's tiring. All day long, I'm sitting singing songs for everyone... but today... It's just felt like... being home, with an old friend. Talking shit. I don't know why but I just feel... comfortable talking with you about... blah. You know? I don't get that much anymore. So, thank you.'

A kiss on the cheek!

OK.

Wait... should I kiss back?

What do I do here?

Has the moment passed?

Yeah... it's passed.

                              ...damn it.

'You're... welcome. Wait, that's stupid. That's not the right response.'

'It's fine Local.'

'No. I mean.... Ditto.'

God, what are you saying you idiot! ABORT, change the subject!

'I mean, me too... I've... it's been really great for me to hang with you too.'

'You are the most adorably awkward human being I've ever met.'

'That's a nice way of saying what I am.'

'Well, I thought borderline sociopathic psychopath was a bit harsh.'

'Harsh, but fair.'

'Nawwww, look at that cute old couple holding hands and sharing an ice cream. Awww they're so sweet! That's real love.'

'Is that the two of us when we're sixty four?'

'You and me?! God no! A miserable mopey bastard like you, I'd kill you within the first year. If you hadn't already strangled me already, that is.'

'I can see that. Especially after one too many of your dud jokes.'

'Exactly. No, we're more your Orpheus &

Eurydice type — doomed from the outset. By this time tomorrow, we'll be glad that we only had twenty four hours to screw up each other's lives.'

...Damn, she's right,

...this really is only going to last a few more hours...

'My feet are killing me, mind if we take a breather?'
  'Course not.'
  'Let's sit on the steps of that church.'
  'St Mary's? Sure.'
  'Ahhh, that's better. Think I'm getting a blister.'
  'Sorry, we have been seeing a lot on foot today.'
  'I've enjoyed it, don't sweat it. Do you want a cigarette?'
  Hmmm... moral quandary.
  I really shouldn't.
  But...
  'Sure. Thanks.... Ahhh.... Forgive me father for I have sinned.'
  'That Catholic guilt sneaking up on you again?'
  'Hmmm. So, religion's never been a part of your life?'
  'Nah.'
  'Nothing huh. Are you spiritual at all?'
  'It would be nice to think there's more to life

than this, of course. But the whole "why are we here?" thing's never really been more than a passing thought.'

'I think about it all the time.'

'Why does that not shock me Local?'

'It scares me to death to think that *this* is it. I mean there's gotta be more to it, you know. There's got to be a bigger reason why we're here. Surely?'

'There was a time when I toyed with it.'

'Christianity?'

'I was contemplating them all, broadly. When I was reflecting on what I was doing with my life.'

'When was that?'

'A... few years ago. When I was considering the longevity of a career choice.'

'Which was?'

'Which was... a conversation for another time and place.'

'What happened to complete and total honesty with a stranger?'

'I never said total.'

'You did.'

'Yeah well... some things are best kept private.'

'And after I told you about Cher!'

'This is true.'

'It's OK, you don't have to tell me if you don't want—'

'—it was when I was briefly escorting.'

Wow.

'Oh OK... Ummm, how did it, I mean how—'

'—How did I get into that?'

'Ahhhh, yeah.'

'It just happened. I wasn't really desperate for money, or touched by an uncle or anything like that. One night... one thing led to another... And it just took on a life of its own from there. There were good days and bad. But I didn't *not* enjoy it.'

'What particularly?'

'The challenge of having to work out a new client very quickly, to make them comfortable. Talking to them, finding out what makes them tick.'

'Wow. That's actually... I'm intrigued by this. Like what were the circumstances... when you started?'

'I was halfway through a biology degree that I wasn't really sure I wanted to finish. And emotionally, I wasn't in the headspace to be in a committed relationship. I didn't feel like going out at night to find random shags, so it was a way to satisfy a need.'

'I find it fascinating that you're telling me all this on the steps of a cathedral.'

'That's what you Catholics do, right? Confess all and hope for absolution.'

'True. So, it was about filling an emotional void?'

'Partially, plus it became a positive distraction to an unfulfilling education. But, you know, I never came from money, so it was always a matter of constantly scrapping together funds to keep the rent paid and the tuition up to date. And I was good at it. I could make four and a half, five a week.'

'Peww. Pounds?'

'Mmm hmm. That set your little Catholic mind spinning?'

'I'm not that pristine. So ummm... how long did

you do it?'

'It was three years give or take. Eventually, I dropped out of school cause it took up all my time.'

'And you stopped because?'

'I got to a point where I realised that apart from not being something I could turn into a lifelong career, I was starting to become detached.'

'What do you mean?'

'You end up living on the edge of society. Waking hours are screwed. When you're with someone and they want to party, you do it too, to keep that connection going. And it helped numb the ones that you really didn't want to be with.'

'Were there a lot of those?'

'Few. So, one day it hit me that this couldn't be my career. I didn't want to go back to my degree. Didn't know what I wanted to do. Maybe teaching, but that didn't seem like the most moral career path to follow next. And it was always gonna be hard to re-enter the workforce and explain the blank space in my resume from 2006-2009 without fudging the truth. So, to answer your question, in a roundabout fashion, it was around that time that I started to look to religion. But none ever clicked.'

'So, what happened?'

'Music. I had a regular who began to teach me simple chords on the guitar, and I really got a high off that. And I was always writing anyway, from a young age — journals, poems, thoughts, whatnot — to keep my mind active... and free. So, I bought this second-hand acoustic Maton, and I ended up playing it loads in my down time. And, I guess I became good at it, not to blow my own trumpet, but I did. I wrote some songs, and I'd play a gig here and there. And then eventually the right people heard. So, doing the first thing helped me get to do what I really wanted, get out and see the world.'

'Do you worry about that, you know, surfacing, becoming public?'

'A little. It's always in the back of my mind. I've put a few subtle hints in my music, so it's never a huge shock if it does. I'm sure it will at some stage, but there's no point hiding it. I figure that the people that it matters to aren't worth having as fans. Can't please everyone, right? But without having done it, I'd never have taken up music and I'd not be here now. I'm not ashamed of it... not really. But I don't talk openly about it.'

'Everything happens for a reason, right?'

'Exactly. Can't buy me love but you can purchase the next closest thing.'

'So... umm, can I ask you a question?'

'Sure.'

'Did you ever spend a week in a Beverly Hills hotel with Richard Gere?'

'Of course, that's part of the training.'

'I mean cause of the whole "Pretty Woman" thing.'

'Yeah, I got your mildly obscure pop cultural reference Local.'

'Oh good.'

Wow.

She was really candid about that.

And, I get the feeling she's never really told a lot of people what she just did.

I like this one.

...I like her a lot.

'How are your feet now?'

'They've stopped barking.'

'Do you want to go check out a bit more of the festival? There's a free concert in the Domain. Some seventeen-piece band from Mexico I think.'

'Sure. Is that down where we saw Marco?'

'Yep, that's the place. You'll know this place like the back of your hand soon.'

'Won't need you anymore, huh?'

'Guess not.'

...I guess not.

This feels right, being with him.

It feels good.

Even though he's nothing like what I would go for.

But maybe that's why I like him so much.

He's this wonderful cocktail of self-hatred and ambivalence.

Like that he cares too much about what others think, but in an empathetic way.

And he's got a cute ass.

And nice hair. Nice hair is an underrated asset.

It's so weird to feel this way, about someone so quickly.

And I know it's a "holiday romance" or whatever you want to call it.

"Instalust"...

But there's something real about him.

He's not putting anything on.

He's exactly what you see.

'Shit.'

'What?'

'Cops. Put your mask on in case they're looking for us from earlier.'

'Which part of earlier?'

'All of it.'

See! That's so endearingly paranoid. But he's genuinely looking out for me.

Or maybe not, maybe he's just protecting himself, and I'm implicit in his sphere of care.

Either way, it's different.

He's different. And I like being here with him.

'Have you heard of these guys? Seventeen-piece Mariachi band from Puebla City.'

'They're amazing.

'Haven't they got a great look.'

'Close your eyes Local.'

'What?'

'Don't watch. Listen.'

And he does.

And he looks so sweet with that little half smile dancing on his lips as he tunes into the sounds.

He's grazing his little finger across my thigh.

Gently.

So, so gently.

I just want to tell him it's OK... you can touch me.

But I know it would embarrass him.

Just leave him to take things at his pace.

There's nowhere else in the world I can think of being right now...

Nowhere.

And we dance, we twist, and shout.
Then he dips me.
I look into his eyes, and he smiles warmly.
And it makes me happy. I'm happy just to dance with him.
I feel happy being with this boy.
And I know he is too.

Then it's all over far too soon.
'We should probably head to your soundcheck.'
'OK.'

Look at her up on stage in that ridiculous superhero costume.
She's so sexy. And beautiful.
She's got such a fantastic voice…
This is a great song.
Grant, what are you doing?!
Am I falling in love with someone I have no chance with?
Again.
You idiot.

'How did that sound Chris?'
'Sounds so good Nina, I might just lift your vocals a bit in the mix though but sounding lovely. Happy Marco?'
'You bet, thanks Nev.'

'Once again Marco, you're amazing, an absolute treasure, truly.'

'I love your music, so it's a breeze. I'm happy to help out.'

'Shall we try "Broken On A Cloudy Day"?'

'Sure. That's that one in A flat minor?'

'Yes, with the reverb.'

'Got it. And 2, 3, 4.'

'Grant.'

'Hey Dave.'

'You surprised me. I was expecting her to be dead and you in jail after an hour.'

'The night's young.'

'Anyway, good job mate. Thank you for helping out. She seemed to have a good day.'

'Do you think?'

''Yeah, she seems pleased... if you overlook the broken wrist.'

'It's not broken.'

'Thankfully. Anyhow, as promised, here's your pay for the job.'

'Thank you. Before I forget, here's a bunch of receipts from the day.'

'Thanks.... She's sounding good.'

'Yeah. Real good. Real good.'

Time check — 7.51.

I wonder if I'll have time to right one more wrong before the day is through?

Or at least try to anyway...

'Dave, I gotta split for a bit OK?'

'Yeah, sure mate. Thanks for helping me out and

showing Nina around.'

'It's been my pleasure.'

I should tell her what I'm doing... but I guess I shouldn't disturb her in the middle of the rehearsal. It's fine. I'll tell Dave.

'Mate, look, can you tell her... ummm, just when you get a chance when she's done, tell her that I really…'

What's the Local up to back there?

Wait, is he… leaving?

Did he just leave?

Really, without a goodbye?

Come on Nina, pull yourself together and stop being stupid. You knew from the outset he was only in this for the money.

How can you now be surprised he's split now he has it?!

It was inevitable.

So why are you upset?

... Although, are you upset?

Hmmm.

Yes, I think... I think I am.

'Incredible Nina. It's gonna be a great show tonight.'

'Thank you Dave. So, ummm, did the Local leave?'

'Who?'

'Ohhh, ummm... Grant, is that his name?'

'Yes. He said to apologise but he had to go and sort something.'

'Right.'

'But he should be back later.'

'OK.'

'So, I've made some calls to Melbourne and they've rounded up the best session muso down there to fill in on guitar tomorrow night. His name's Ray something. I wrote it down.'

'That's fine. Thanks for that. I'll just get through tonight and then start panicking about tomorrow though.'

'Fair enough. So, look we're all going to grab a bite just up the road if you want to join us?'

'Actually... I think I'll head back to the hotel. Take a quick nap. I've gotta change out of this anyway.'

'You're not gonna take the stage as Wonder Woman?'

'Maybe next time.'

'I'll hold you to that. OK, well you rest up. Been a long day I'll bet.'

'Mmmm, sure has.'

'OK, well, see you in a few hours.'

'A few hours, sure.'

'You know, he will be back. He should be anyway.'

'It's OK, it doesn't really bother me either way.'

Though I'm quite sure that he won't be back.

And I'm quite sure that it does bother me.

Why do I feel worse about him leaving —

someone I knew for twelve hours — than being dumped by someone I was dating for three years?!
Madness.
Pull yourself together woman!
Pull yourself together....

CHAPTER SIXTEEN

EIGHT PM

KNOCK KNOCK KNOCK.

'Coming.'

Hope for the best…

…prepare for the worst.

'What the hell are you doing here?!'

'Hey sis.'

'This oughta be good. Well, go on then, what's the story? Why aren't you on a plane right now?'

'I missed my flight.'

'How the fuck, pardon my French, did you miss your flight? I dropped you at the terminal two hours before departure?'

'They ruled me a flight risk… because I was intoxicated.'

'Of course you were. Jesus! Can you not do anything right?! I should have known better than to not walk you on the plane myself. And now explain why you're dressed as an ass clown in that superhero get up?'

Oh yeah, I forgot I was still in the stupid

costume.

Probably not the impression I was hoping to make.

'It's typical Grant. Just fucking typical, you look like a fucking mess, you can't even get on a plane when you're dropped at the tarmac. Unbelievable. When are you going to grow up?!'

I deserved that.

'This is for you Blue.'

'What is it? And don't call me Blue, you know I can't stand it.'

'It's my pay from a job I took today. It's not all the money I owe you, but it's a start.'

'A job? What job?'

'I was chaperoning a musician around town.'

'They let you do that again after what happened last time?'

'They were desperate.'

'They must have been. Well… anyway… thank you for this.'

'I couldn't leave Sydney with things the way they were between us…'

'It could have gone better.'

'I'm so sorry Em. For everything. I…'

Gotta find the words.

The better words, the ten dollar words to say how incredibly sorry I am.

That I know how much I've fucked up.

But maybe this silence between us says it all.

'Come here, and give me a hug, you buggar.'

And I do.

And we both start to cry, as she holds me tight.

I've missed this. Her huge, enveloping hugs.

I've missed that goofy guffaw too.

I've missed her.

'I just miss her, so fucking much Grant. Every single day.'

'I know.'

'I thought today would be OK, you know? That enough time's passsed that I wouldn't be a complete wreck. But it's floored me.'

'I shouldn't have left you to deal with it alone today. I'm so sorry. It was selfish of me.'

'Look… I'm sorry also for driving off at the airport. That wasn't fair. And for the moods I've been in. And for blaming you. It was wrong. I was wrong to blame you. It wasn't your fault. It was an accident.'

'I know.'

'For what it's worth… thank you for coming back.'

'Thank you for not kicking my ass.'

'Ha! I never said I wasn't gonna do that.'

'Don't think cause you're my sister I won't fight back.'

'You did always want to fight dirty.'

'I learnt it from the best.'

'So kind of you to say.'

'Ain't no thang. Oh hey, that reminds me… did you hear what happened when they started showing the Flintstones in the United Arab Emirates?'

'No, what?'

'They don't really like it in Dubai but they do in Abu-Dhabi.'

'Huh?'

'Oh damn it, I screwed up the punchline.'

'You idiot.'

'Massive idiot.

There she is... the girl who's been absent for so long, my older sister...

'So, you're still going away?'

'Yeah, tomorrow morning?'

'Do you need another lift?'

'No, I should be alright to get there this time.'

'You sure? I can make sure you actually get on the plane this time?'

'Ha. I'm good. Ain't it strange what a difference a day can make.'

'You said it.'

'So what are you up to? Where's Matt?'

'Jack's got him tonight. So, I've been left to get things ready for his birthday party tomorrow. Twenty five screaming rugrats from ten in the morning. What a treat!'

'Wow, got your hands full.'

'And then some.'

'Do you want some help?'

'I thought you'd never ask. Come on in.'

'Would you mind signing this one for my sister too please, Nina?'

'Of course.'

'I *ADORE* your first album. I listened to it on repeat for like two years in high school. Actually almost three, I think.'

'You're quite the dedicated fan.'

'It helped me with so, so much I was going through.'

'That's really nice to hear things like that. Makes

this all feel like I'm really connecting with people. Here you go.'

'Thank you sooooo much.'

'You're welcome. Bye.'

And off I go, continuing to wander the streets of Sydney.

Think I'll keep my head down to avoid any more recognition though. I can't handle it right now....

I just want to go home.

London home.

Like right now.... I just want to be in my bed.

Eating crisps… those cool ranch ones.

And tubs of Savoy truffle ice cream.

And I don't want to leave bed for five days.

In fact, if I died in bed after those five days and they found me under a layer of Doritos dust, I'd have perished a happy woman.

Maybe I should just quit, get a bunch of cats and await my inevitable cool ranch-flavoured doom.

Worse ways to go, right?

Just feel so… hollow inside right now.

All these happy couples… and families. I can't deal with your joy tonight.

...I wonder what Pete's doing right now?

Would it hurt, really, to call him... and talk through what happened?

Why we broke up and all that?

A final calm analysis of what went wrong?

That couldn't hurt.

Could it...?

...no.

NO NO NO NO NO NO!

NO!

You wanted it to end.

And it has, so sit with it.

You just didn't think you'd feel so empty about it…

But it's to be expected, right? You can't just assume every feeling you have about someone to leave your body straight away.

You know this.

So put that rat out of your mind.

You've gotta go through all the shit feelings to come back…

Trust the process.

One thing's for certain, I'm never touring for this long ever again.

I'm so over seeing everyone back home on Facebook and Instagram, laying foundations for life.

I'm happy you got married.

I'm glad your baby is healthy.

I'm really pleased that you bought a house.

But I want that.

I want that stability.

I want that boringness.

…I want to come home to someone.

…why did I tell him about my past?

I knew it would scare people off.

Stupid, Nina.

So

fucking
stupid.

'You know I don't think I've made a cake —
birthday or otherwise — in like... forever. Maybe
biscuits that one time with grandma.'
'You've never been the most domesticated catch,
little brother.'
'You always had mum to learn all her tips from.'
'You could have picked those up too, you know.
You just spent too much time with dad.'
'Maybe... but this is... I like this. This is fun.'
'If you're enjoying it so much, you can stay here
and cook two different meals every night and I'll
run off to Amsterdam. OK?'
'Nah, you're right.'
'Thought as much.'
'So, ummm... speaking of him, I think... ahh, I
think the old man might be back in town.'
'You saw him?'
'No. I was... out there... at the spot today, a
couple of hours ago. I could just tell that he'd been
there. You remember that story about the Beatles'
album?'
'Yeah.'
'A copy of it was left near that railing that he
carved into.'
'Right.'
'Em... you OK?'
Just like that, the rage within her went from
zero to a hundred and sixty in two point seven
seconds.

'You, I get. It was stupid youth, fixing a hole in your life and not knowing what to do. I didn't like when you did it, I didn't like when you went off the rails, but in a way, I could understand it. But him... For him to just disappear like nothing happened. You know... GOD DAMN HIM! I'm so SOOOOO pissed off with him. To just abandon us both like that as if he was the only one feeling anything. She would have been so angry at him for leaving, so incredibly angry. FUCK!'

SMASH.

And the bag of lollies she launched at the wall, shatters across the floor.

'Come here sis.'

'I'm so mad at him.'

'I know. You and I both.'

'How could he do it?'

'I don't know... But I want to say something that's gone a long time unsaid. You held it together and I'm sincerely grateful cause otherwise we would have fallen apart as a family. Thank you for being the rock when neither he or I would be.'

'I always said I was stronger than you.'

'And you proved it.'

'I love you Grant. I really do.'

'I love you too sis.'

'God, I made a meal of that lolly bag, didn't I?'

'Where's the dustpan and broom?'

'Leave it, I'll do.'

'No, I've got it. Is it under the sink?'

'Just where mum would keep hers.'

'Ha, thought so.'

'Thanks.'

'So, ummm. You know that motorbike of

Jack's.'

'Yeah?'

'Has he still got it?'

'He's still trying to sell it. Well, he wants to keep it, but it's just gathering dust in the shed. I've told him if he doesn't offload it soon, I'll dump it in the harbour. Why?'

'How much does he want for it?'

'You looking to make me an offer, little brother?'

'Maybe… very possibly maybe.'

CHAPTER SEVENTEEN

NINE PM

What time is it?

9.20.

So, I got in thirty minutes kip. Better than nothing, I suppose.

Alright, so get up, do the show, keep it tight and quick, then leave straight away afterwards.

No autographs.

No after parties.

Just go to bed.

Fall asleep.

Wake up and be one day closer to being home.

You can do this.

You can do it.

Hmmmm, what to wear?

It was gonna be the red thingy with the long sleeves, but that's not happening with my wrist all bandaged up.

Wear the black one again I guess.

Pee-yew… it could do with a wash…

…will have to do it tomorrow though, haven't

got time to faff about with anything else.

Cheeky squirt of Febreeze should conceal it for the time being though.

Quick shower to wake me up?

Have I got time?

Yeah, always time for a shower.

Doo dee de dah doooo.

Ahhh, at least they've got the water pressure perfect. I've lost count how many hotels have terrible water press—

—KNOCK KNOCK.

'Driver Miss.'

Oh god.

'Ahhhh, I'm not ready. I'm in the shower. Come back in twenty minutes.'

Why's he so early? I said to have them meet me downstairs.

Anyway, where's the soap?

Over on the basin? Really?

Can't they get organised enough to just stick a cake of soap in the shower so you can use it there —

—KNOCK KNOCK KNOCK

Grrrrrrr.

'I SAID I'M NOT READY!'

Just go and wait downstairs. He's ruining my shower!

KNOCK KNOCK KNOCK KNOCK.

Not smart buddy. Not smart at all!

Where's the towel?

Right, that's it.

'Are you deaf I said I'm not ready!

'Driver Miss.'

Now I've gotta open the door to bite his head

off!

'I SAID…!'

'Surprise!'

'Oh... it's you!'

He came back!

EEK!!!

'It *is* me. And your chariot awaits.'

'I didn't think... I mean.... I thought you left... but you came back.'

'Was it ever in question?'

'I… thought maybe after what I told you earlier… on the steps about my past… that… well I thought you'd done a runner.'

'You're gonna have to try a little harder than that to shake me.'

'Well, look, as you can see, I'm nowhere near ready… I've only just got out of the shower.'

'That I can definitely see. And you've never looked better.'

'What? Oh, yes... I forgot about your fetish for women in towels.'

'More a preference than a fetish, per se.'

'Regardless, I still have to get ready so why don't you wait for me downstairs in the lobby, OK Romeo?'

'No problem. I'll just wait downstairs.'

'Good, you do that.'

'OK, I'm going downstairs now. I'll just be waiting down at the bottom of the stairs.'

'Downstairs. Yes, there's a good lad.'

'I'll be down those stairs. Those ones just over there. Down, not up mind you, downstairs. So you know where to find me?'

'Upstairs right got it.'

'No, no, downstairs.'

'Roger.'

'No, Grant. Do you think maybe I should draw you a map of where I'll be?'

'I think I should be OK. It's upstairs, right?'

'No, no, down. Downstairs. How about I come in and draw you a map? Might be best.'

'Just go! I'll be up soon.'

'Down!'

'Down down, yes down. BYE!'

Silly boy.

Silly cute boy.

It's odd that she seemed so shocked that I came to get her.

I guess Dave mustn't have passed on my message that I'll be back.

Still, she must have realised that I wouldn't just leave without saying goodbye.

…Unless.

Fuck.

Of course!

She would have seen me get paid and thought that I've got what I needed from the day and split.

Damn.

Although... it's nice to think that she must have missed me, even just a little, to be so surprised I returned.

Guess I must have made some impression.

She's sure made one on me.

What a day.

Never in my wildest thoughts would I have

imagined it would turn out this way.

She's… everything I've never known I was looking for in a person.

She's the "you" I've been looking for.

…why's life deal shit like this out when I'm probably never gonna see her again after tonight?

'I'm ready.'

'Oh, you startled me.'

'Startled? What are you, a ninety year old woman? Who says "startled" these days?'

'OK, settle down Roget. I was gonna give you this gas station rose that I got while I was waiting, but if you're gonna keep mocking me at every opportunity.'

'Naw, aren't you sweet, did you buy this for me?'

'No, I found it in the trash out back. YES, of course I did. So, have you got everything? Don't need a guitar?'

'No —OOOH, and the great thing is the airline found my other guitar, it had gone to Melbourne. So I told them to hold it there, and I'll grab it tomorrow.'

'Melbourne huh, fancy that.'

'Terrific stroke of luck. So, shall we?'

'Yes.'

'Which car is yours?'

'Ahhh, actually it's this.'

'A green Kawasaki Ninja. Sweet!'

'You don't mind?'

'Have you met me before?! Hop on before I take it for a spin myself.'

'Here's your helmet. Ready?'

'Do it!'

Time check — 9.47.

The gig starts at 10.15.

I have Nina Taylor on the back of this newly acquired motorbike.

Everything is under control.

Everything is good.

Everything is very good.

CHAPTER EIGHTEEN
TEN PM

'We love you Nina!'

'WOOO HOOO!'

'Thank you guys, thank you so much.'

'YEAH!'

'Thank you. So, I must apologise about tonight's performance. I think you may have noticed — that is, the eagle-eyed amongst you may have noticed — that I'm not playing guitar tonight. I had a little *faux pas* earlier today.'

'AWWWWWW!'

'Thank you for that feigned pity guys, I'll remember it fondly as I'm writing my review on TripAdvisor after the show for the Sydney Opera House "Love the architecture, but beware of dancing on its steps as it's a disaster waiting to happen... Or something". But anyway, despite how this mildly sprained wrist looks, I'll live, so you can cut that "AWWWWing" out right now. But before I go into the next song, tonight came together with a little help from my friends, so I want to introduce you to just an absolutely beautiful soul. My new hero and the wind beneath my wings — too much? Too much, OK — but the lovely fellow without whom I would have had to cancel the show, so please give it up for Marco Reid.'

'WOOOOO!!!'

'YEAH MARC-OOOOO!!!'

'Thank you Marco, sincerely. OK, so this next song, I want to dedicate it to Sydney.'

'WOOOOOO!'

'Today was my first time here, my first experience here, and it's exceeded all expectations, which were admittedly high from what I'd been told about it. It's truly a beautiful city — despite what some of you may think — and it's really been magical. I love it. So thank you Sydney.'

'YYEAHHHHH'

'WOOOOOO!'

'MOVE HERE NINA!!!'

'I very well may when the tour ends. Haha, but this next song is quite new. In fact, it was just written today so you may have to bear with me as I really only know about half the words. But Grant, wherever you are out there... here's to ticking things off lists. This is called "My Ephemeral Heart".'

Holy shit! She's gonna sing it!
Here!!
This is..
...it could be a nightmare actually....
 Oh my god, what did I write, if I knew she'd

167

sing it now, I would have spent much longer on the lyrics.
Oh shit...
...here it goes....

"The toy soldier in the Emerald City,
Lost when his corp fell apart,
Believing if any girl loved the Beatles
She'd break his clockwork heart
The ballerina trapped in her music box
From a kingdom so far away
Worn out from spinning around the world
Seeing night but never the day
Yet we find ourselves here in this moment
In this dream if from which we do wake
It will cause My Ephemeral Heart
To break.
Missed connections and stolen vodka
Jumping ship and running away
Sightseeing in a virtual daydream
Never made so much from one single day
Am I reading the signs right?
Is this more than one way?
Is there a chance of tomorrow?
Or just twenty-four hours at play?
Can we simply just live in this moment?
That is ours and that no one can take.
That way My Ephemeral Heart
You'll never break.
Is this the start of forever?
Does it all change here, no delay?
Or am I counting the seconds to goodbye
To the one who got away?
So let's live here in this moment

let it be whatever we make.
Because Your Ephemeral Heart,
I never want to break."

'Thank you.'

Holy.
Fucking.
Shit.
If I live a thousand lifetimes, nothing will ever top that.
WOOOOOOOOOOOOO!!!!!!!
YESSSS!!!!
AGAIN!!!!!
Wow.
Blown away.
Just... that was incredible... wow.

'But I'm with the band.'
   'Where's your pass then?'
   'I don't have one, but my name should be on the list, under Revolver, Grant Ryder.'
   'Hmmmmm.... Nope, nothing here. No pass, no list, no entry.'
   'But I'm part of the crew, I was with Nina all day— HEY DAVE!! Come over here.'
   'What's up?'
   'Why aren't I on the list?'
   'Oh, sorry, forgot.'
   'You forgot a bunch of stuff.'

'Yeah Oli, Grant's with us, let him through.'

'OK, let me stamp you.'

'Thanks. Hey Dave, where's Marco?'

'He should be at the back of the stage, just around those boxes.'

'OK, thanks.'

'You sticking around for a drink?'

'I'm staying for a bit.'

But not for a drink.

OK, so where is he... ahhh, there he is, packing up his guitars.

'Hey Marco.'

'Hi Grant.'

'Mate, that was astounding. Amazing work. I always knew you were great, but that show was off the charts.'

'Thanks mate. She's something though, right? Thank you for thinking of me for the gig.'

'There's not a single person who could have done it better. Here, I got you a beer.'

'Thanks, cheers, oh, where's yours?'

'Yeah, I'm thinking I might try not drinking for a while. Properly. See how it suits me.'

'I'll drink to that.'

'I've got something else for you. Here.'

'Keys? What are these for?'

'For the Kawasaki out in the back lane. I know it's not a car but... it's something to apologise for what I did to yours, until, you know, I can repay you properly for it.'

'Really?'

'The bike will be more use to you than me anyway. Sell it, keep it, whatever you need to.'

'Oh, mate. Bring it in for the hug.'

'Oh OK.'

'Thank you mate. I appreciate the gesture.'

'Better late than never.'

'For sure. Look I've gotta pack up now, I'm heading over to catch the end of Father John Misty at the Metro.'

'Of course mate. Anyway, look I just wanted to say sorry again. For what I caused. And for not connecting with you again sooner. I leave tomorrow morning, but if it's cool, I'd like to stay in touch, if that's OK?'

'You better mate. Please don't be a stranger this time, OK?'

'OK.'

'And please... look after yourself mate. Don't let me down.'

'I won't. I promise you.'

And we hug, knowing it may be the last time our paths ever cross.

'See you round mate.'

'Thanks Marco.'

Well, I wasn't expecting it at all, but that became one of the best shows I've done on this tour.

It was so liberating just concentrating on singing and having someone else on guitar... may have stumbled upon a winning formula.

But the look on the Local's when I sang the song was... I'll never forget that.

It was definitely worth a twisted wrist.

Where is he though? I thought he'd be waiting at the bar like we discussed — oooh, there he is.

'Woooooo, encore encore bravo encore!'

"Thank you Local, thank you, you're too kind.'

'That was... WOW! I was absolutely blown away.'

'So you liked it huh? I messed up a few songs though especially "The House That Guilt Built".'

'No one noticed for a second. You were amazing. Ohhh, and that song — our song! I can't believe you wrote that music and arranged it all so quickly.'

'It was super, super rough. I'll work on it more at a later stage... but I wanted to sing it tonight. From me to you.'

'Well... I guess you could call that romantic. Cheesy as fuck... but, you know, romantic.'

'Smart arse.'

'However, I will say that if that song makes it big — which it's bound to, how could it not?! — I'll want my share of the royalties!'

'Ha, you'll have to track me down first.'

'Challenge accepted.'

'Do you want to grab a seat?'

'Sure, but don't you have to do anymore signings or anything?'

'No, not really.'

'OK, well there's a booth just there.'

'How convenient.'

'But seriously, like how did you come up with that melody so quickly, I'm really amazed.'

'It was just a simple chord progression. Plus, I had to fudge a few lines here and there and make a few structural changes to get it to rhyme.'

'Yeah but you somehow made it even better because of that.'

'Just comes with experience of knowing how to arrange a song. Marco actually helped bring it to life more than I did to be completely honest.'

'I wish I'd known about your music a year ago. You capture the feel of tortured love so well.'

'What's the point of a painful past if you can't use it to inspire some kind of artistic output?'

'Your songs definitely seemed very personal.'

'There's truth to that. Mostly they're a reflection of the end of several relationships. I find that when I'm with someone, it's a distraction — the best kind, but a distraction none the less. But no one who's truly happy ever gets anything done. And no one really wants to hear "I'm so happy, life's so great". That's what music's for, to remind us all that love stinks.'

'Ha!'

'What? It's true.'

'I know. It's just interesting hearing from someone who makes a living from it.'

'Thing I figure is that everyone's had their heart broken. Not everyone can say they've experienced love though. So that means heartbreak is the universal condition, moreso than love.'

'That's interesting.'

'We have more time to listen to each other's stories of falling out of love than of falling in it.'

'I've never thought about that. It's true, we all know more about loss than love.'

I love the sparkle in his eye as he's thinking about that.

I need to remember this night.

I need to remember him.

Where's my phone?

'What are you doing?'

'Capturing the moment.'

'Are you filming?'

'Yes.'

'Ha, stop it.'

'No, I want proof you that existed. I don't want to wake up tomorrow and think it was all a dream.'

'A nightmare sounds more likely. OK, well, that's enough. You got me. Now, cut it out.'

'No. Tell me something.'

'Tell you what?'

'Tell me... I know, tell me what you thought when you first saw me this morning.'

'This morning, jeez... OK, well, at the airport when I first saw you I guess... I thought you were... pretty.'

'Nice. But come on, you can do better than that.'

'OK... well, when I first saw you.... Put it this way, I would never have had the tenacity to get up and speak to you if I wasn't leaving this city and never seeing you again. Because you were too pretty.'

'And are you glad?'

'What, that I did speak to you?'

'Yes.'

'I don't know whether glad covers it…'

And that's when I saw her, standing there.

Oh.

Fuck.

At literally the worst possible moment in the history of someone approaching someone, she approaches me.

She always kinda had shit timing.

'Hey Grant.'

'Hey.'

'How are you?'

'Yeah. I'm OK. You?'

'I'm doing really well thanks.'

'Good... ummmm, surprised to find you here. At this show.'

'Are you kidding? I'm a huge fan, Nina. You were amazing tonight.'

'Oh, thank you so much.'

'I'm Abigail.'

'Oh, Abigail... it's nice to meet you.'

And this is where the awkward silence envelops the room...

'I'm just gonna grab a drink, do you want a beer Local, I'll get you one?'

'No, thanks.'

'OK. I'll be back in a tick.'

'Do you mind if I sit?'

'Sure.'

'So... how are you doing? Really?'

'Well, you know... been better.'

'I heard that you were moving overseas?'

'Who told you that?'

'I heard it around.'

'It's weird seeing you. Here at this gig, I mean.'

'Grant, I was constantly trying to get you to listen to her music.'

'Right. I don't recall that.'

'Hmmmm. And so... you know her?'

'I umm, kinda... not really, it's a long story.'

'OK. Look... I never had the chance to say this before, I couldn't find a time that wasn't going to

be seen as poor timing but... I'm really sorry that...
well, the way everything went down. With the
breakup, and your mum.'

'Yeah, well, what can you do, you know.'

'I'm just sorry I couldn't be there... When she
died... I felt so so terrible that I couldn't do
anything for you, but it just didn't seem right to be
there.'

'I guess we all have decisions to make.'

I'm not sure if I'm coming across as Arcticly cold
as I feel right now.

...or whether I even want to.

'Look, I don't know whether this is the right
time or place to tell you this, but I think maybe it's
best you hear it from me rather than someone else.'

'What?'

'...I'm getting married.'

And there it is.

The big ring on her finger that she self-
consciously pulled behind her back to avoid my
stare.

'Right. Great. Well that's excellent news isn't it?
I'm very VERY happy for you.'

'Grant... you can't have expected me to not
move on. It's been over a year since we broke up
—'

'—It's been three hundred and sixty seven days
actually, but who's counting.'

'I shouldn't have said anything—'

'—No, no, I mean it, congratulations.'

'I'm gonna go. I'm sorry for bringing it up.'

'No point wasting any time huh? Get me out the
door and move right onto the next one. Here's to a
very happy life for you both. Tell me, who's the

lucky guy huh?'

'Goodbye Grant.'

And there's that trusty old feeling of being kicked in the guts again.

Welcome back, old friend.

'Are you OK? Grant?'

'Uhh.'

'Are you OK?'

I love a good rhetorical question, because he looks far from OK.

'Sorry, yeah. I'm living the dream! Woo!'

'Was that the first time you've seen her, since it ended?'

'Yeah, it's been a while... so much so that she's moved on completely and she's getting married.'

'Oh. That sucks.'

'That it does, that it does.'

'Hey, I was thinking, maybe we should get outta here. Do you want to get out of here?'

'Yeah… Let's go somewhere… anywhere but here.'

'OK, I'll grab my things. Just wait here, OK.'

'Yeah, sure... What the fuck?! She's with him!! THAT FUCKING ARSEHOLE!'

'What? Who?'

'Over at the coatcheck. Abigail is with *him*. You are kidding me. HIM!?!'

'WHO?!'

'That prick we got weed off this morning.'

'Bill?'

'Yeah… Oh, I've gotta find out about this!'

'Grant, just stay here. Please don't do anything stupid.'

'Oi!'

'Oh shit.'

'You're fucking kidding me, Abigail. Him?! This drug dealing low life.'

'Shit, Grant. Sorry buddy it's—'

'Shut up. Just shut up Bill.'

'Grant, I'm sorry you found out this way—'

'—When did this glorious union begin?'

'Bill, let's just go.'

'How long! You're marrying him after a year, I don't buy it. Was this happening when we were together?'

'We're over Grant. I moved on. You should have too. Let's go Bill.'

'That's it, just fuck right off you two junkies.'

'Grant, cut it out OK. It's over, they've gone. Just... let it go.'

'I seriously can't believe it. I'm so angry right now.'

'I know it must sting, but maybe it's for the best that you found out. Now you know, and you can, in time, let it slide.'

'Oh, I'm not good enough for her, but... but, that guy, THAT's her Prince Charming.'

'I know this is the last thing you want to hear right now, but at least you have some closure now, y'know, ob la di ob la dah, life goes on and all that —'

'—Look, I've had enough platitudes from you today. All this, all of it is cause of you, and my stupid idea to help you.'

'Hey, just calm down OK. You're getting real

close to saying something you're going to regret.'

'Regret! I regret sitting in the same food court as you this morning. All I wanted to do today was get on a bloody plane and put this place as far behind me as possible. And now I've been dragged through this city by the ghost of Christmas past.'

'I get it. Today was not easy for you. It has and will always have real significance. Not just because of your mum. But what happened has passed. And no matter what you try, you can't change that. You have to find something to get you through another day.'

'It's that easy for you, isn't it? Wake up and start again. It's only love, right? Turn all the mishaps from the day, week, *year* before into fodder for the next album of "woe is me" heartache? Some of us actually feel things, not as an excuse to live like a bleeding heart to improve record sales.'

'You're acting like a little child. It's all "I, me, mine" with you.'

Am I finally seeing his true side?

Is this the real him?

If it is, I don't like it.

And I can see exactly why she left him.

'Are you putting any thought into the words coming out of that hole in your face? Or are you opening it and hoping for the worst?'

'Truth hurts huh?'

'Well here's the truth. You've got your money from taking me around now, so why don't you go and take yer blues and piss it up a wall? No sense breaking the habit of a lifetime for my expense.'

'That is the single best plan you've had all day.'

'You know what, there's not a damned thing

wrong with this city. You're just too pig-headed to think it owes you something. So, run away and hope it solves all your problems, but you want to know something, from someone who's tried it her whole life — anywhere you go, there you are.'

'If I wanted advice like that, I'd consult a fortune cookie. Do I get my lucky number next?'

Fuck... how did this turn so quickly.

Come on Nina, find a way to bring him back from this.

'This is not you Grant. I saw a version of you today that's real. Please, please don't be this person. I'm looking through you and I want to tell you that you're not this person.'

'What do you know about me? You've known me twelve hours and you're expert on my feelings.'

Just apologise Grant...

I'm not going to say it but please just look in my eyes and see what I'm telling you...

...Please.

Don't be this person Grant.

Just look at my eyes.

'Grant, if you can't let go of the past, how can you ever face the future?'

'I can't deal with this. I'm outta here. Goodbye.'

...It's not going to happen.

And just like that, he walks out of my life.

Dumped twice in one day.

That's a new record Nina, you're doing great.

Really super duper...

Who does she think she is, telling me this isn't me?!

She doesn't know me. What, because we shared an ice cream on the steps of the Opera House we're kindred soulmates?!

Pfff.

I'm so fucking angry right now I can't think straight.

I can't rationalise any of this.

It just... it just doesn't compute. It's... all too much.

Where the fuck am I going?

I need a drink. Only thing that will change this situation right now.

Lots and lots and copious amounts of alcohol.

'TAXI!'

Fuck.

'Oiii, TAXI!'

Why didn't you stop, you jerk!

Where's the taxi rank? Over there—

—Is that Abigail and Bill waiting at it?

Right, I need answers.

'Oi! Come here you.'

'Grant, just go away. Go home.'

'How long has this been going on Bill?!'

'Grant, go home... or I'll call security over.'

'I don't care. How long has this been happening?'

'Calm down mate!'

"HOW LONG!'

'Two and half years OK!'

'If we're gonna have this out Ryder, why don't we do it in the road, away from these people?'

And before I can even form the thought about how good it would be to break his nose, my clenched fist swings at it.

And just as quickly, his fist connects with my head.

Then it all goes black.

CHAPTER NINETEEN

ELEVEN PM

'Welcome back from your golden slumber, Mr Ryder. How are you feeling?'

'I feel fine, thank you nurse.'

...if you discount the cocktail of shame, anger and regret currently swimming through my head, I'm perfectly "fine".

'Would you like some water?'

...that should fix everything.

'Yes please.'

'Now that you're awake, there's a couple of police officers who need to speak with you, about filing charges against the man that hit you.'

'No, no that's not happening. There's no need.'

'I'm not sure you have a choice. With the one-punch rule Sydney has, it's mandatory.'

'I wasn't punched. I fell.'

'Into a fist?'

'I tripped on a… stone. I'm a klutz. Two left feet.'

'Hmmm. Well, in that case, I'll let them know

that it was an accident.'

And just when I think the day can't get any worse, I've just seen a face I did not want to see today.

'Rough night?'

'You could say that.'

'And you are?'

'I'm his father.'

'And will you be taking him home?'

'Yes.'

'NO!'

'You need someone to escort you out of here tonight, Mr Ryder.'

'Why?'

'Hospital policy.'

'I'll take care of him thank you nurse."

'Well, I'll leave you two. Just keep that bump iced up for the next few hours.'

'So, the prodigal father returns. Why are you even here?'

'I heard you were hit.'

'But how did you know?'

'Emily told me.'

Great, thanks sis.

'Look, it's been great catching up. A real blast. I really appreciate you spending your valuable time, but I've gotta split. We must do this again in about twenty five years. Enjoy your trip back to the USSR or wherever you've been. But this bird has flown. Bye.'

'Grant, just wait up.'

'No.'

Listen legs, I don't ask much of you, but just this once get me out those sliding doors as fast as you can.

'Come on, slow down!'

'Just go away. I have nothing to say to you.'

'You shouldn't be out by yourself after that knock. Just come back to my place and rest. We can talk. Or not talk, whatever you want.'

'I'll pass thanks.'

'I know I can't fix things in one night. But I'd really like if you'd come back. Even if only for a short while.'

'And I would have really liked — given the circumstances of the last year — if you'd stuck around, you know, made sure your kids were OK. But we don't always get what we want do we?'

'I deserve that.'

'Do you think she would have wanted you to fuck off and leave us alone?! To deal with it by ourselves? Do you think she wanted that?'

'I'm sorry. I was angry. More than you'll ever understand.'

'With who?'

'Everyone.'

'With me?'

Go on.

Say it.

You know you want to.

Say you were angry as hell with me.

'I was angry with everyone.'

'And are you still angry?'

'No. I've moved past it.'

'Well, I'm pleased you came around eventually.

Glad you've found peace. What the fuck is wrong with you?! I can't believe you could possibly think that that was OK to just leave...You know what? Forget it... what's the point in having it out now? What's done is done. I really can't be bothered going over it again. Not bothered in the slightest.'

Well, in that case, Grant, just leave.

Walk away.

Just put one foot in front of the other and go…

…Or completely ignore your inner voice and keep having it out with him.

'Actually. Fuck it. And fuck you. With what you did, you can stand there and listen to me. Stand there and I swear to god if a single sound comes out of your mouth, I don't even want to think what I'll do.'

Breathe Grant, just get it all out.

'You don't get to leave. That's not the way it works. From the moment you make the decision to have me, to have Emily — you don't get to leave. You're a fucking coward. You never even asked if I needed someone. Mum would hate you for it. I get it, I fucked up, big time. If it wasn't for me, mum would still be... she'd still be here... It's my fault and I have to live with that, I have to carry that weight... But it's your job to tell me it's not my fault. It was your job to help me pick up the pieces.'

'I'm so sorry Grant. I was so angry with you for what happened that… I couldn't face you. But I know it's not your fault. I always knew it wasn't. But I couldn't face the life she'd left behind.'

And because I don't know what else to do, I fall into his arms.

And the tears fall effortlessly onto his shoulder, while my back catches some of his.

And then it all comes flooding back and I remember this.

I remember what his embrace feels like.

The safety of it.

But no…

…no no no.

He doesn't get instant forgiveness.

Not after everything that passed.

'Let go of me.'

'OK. Where are you going now?'

'To buy cigarettes.'

Great, he's following me.

'Pack of Marlboro Gold.'

'Thirty four dollars please.'

'Jesus… here.'

'I thought you'd quit.'

'What can I say, it's been a shit of a day.'

'A hard day's night?'

'And then some.'

Ahhhh, nicotine, my old friend.

'Can I have one?'

'You don't smoke.'

'What can I say, it's been a shit of a year.'

'Fine, here.'

'Thanks.'

Pfft — he smokes like a fucking child.

Has no idea what he's doing.

'So now what? We stand in the street and stare at each other chuffing back darts?'

'I have a bottle of Laphroaig and some Chinese

leftovers at mine. It's not far,   down on BlueJay
Way.'
  'Are you trying to win me over with cold rice?'
  'How am I doing?'
  'Terribly.'
  He's made the effort to find me…
  …and we need to have this out at some stage.
  No point delaying the inevitable I guess.
  'Fine, lead the way.'

CHAPTER TWENTY

TWELVE AM

'Here's your whiskey.'

  'Don't want one.'

  'Oh.'

  'Can I have some water?'

'Are you sure?'

'There's nothing I'd like more right now than to snatch that bottle from your hand and neck it, especially being here, doing this… but water is what I need.'

  'OK.'

  Christ, look at this makeshift shrine he's laid out for her.

  Ha, that photo was taken at Jervis Bay on that holiday when I was like five… or was it six? It was when those kids stole my bike, and it turned up buried under the caravan.

  Their wedding photo… he was definitely punching above his weight there.

  And is that… it *is*. The infamous torn up "Sgt. Pepper's" album sleeve. I'm amazed that he still has it.

'Here.'

'Thanks.'

'See you've found that relic from a past life. Did I ever tell you the story of how we got kicked out of a record store when your mum tore up that very cover?'

'Once or twice.'

'Oh.'

'So… we saw you'd been out there today. Left another copy?'

'Who saw? You and Em?'

'No, just… it was no one. Someone I just met.'

'Interesting place to take someone you just met.'

...And the silence settles uncomfortably on the balcony.

Guess I'll just look out over the Harbour from this Point Piper apartment.

This view's pretty spectacular though.

'Good view huh?'

'I guess.'

'So… Amsterdam?'

'Hmmm.'

'Is this "no one" going with you?'

'No. She's not… It's nothing like that. Nothing's happening anyway after what happened tonight.'

'It can get pretty cold over there. In Amsterdam.'

'I'll make sure I get a warm jacket.'

'A jacket won't keep you warm from that kind of chill.'

…It's taking literally every ounce of will power to not grab that bottle of whiskey right now.

'Can you put the bottle away? Please.'

'Sure.'

Outta sight, outta mind... I hope.

'So, how long are you in town for this time?'

'I thought I'd take some time off work. Stick around a while. See if this warmer climate still suits me.'

'I know what you're doing, but you're laying on the subtext pretty thick there, old man.'

'Sorry.'

'It's alright... Em's majorly pissed with you. I'm furious, but she's ballistic.'

'I know.... I spoke with her earlier. She's already read me section one of her riot act. It was a doozy.'

'What did she say?'

'She said... she said... well, you can imagine.'

'Well as someone once told me, all women are a little bit crazy, right?'

'Ha. Who told you that?'

'You did.'

'Me?'

'Was one of the only two pieces of advice you ever thought necessary to pass on about women.'

'I don't think I would have said that.'

'I guarantee it was you.'

'What was the other?'

'Other what?'

'Piece of advice about women.'

'Something about Beatles and heartbreak.'

And this guides both our hands subconsciously to pick up a corner of the torn album cover.

I got Buster Keaton, he gets Bob Dylan.

And as we turn them through our fingers, somehow the silence becomes comfortable.

...I've never noticed that I have his nose.

Same flat bridge.

'You know getting your heart broken isn't the worst thing in the world.'

'I know.'

'You're probably past the point of taking advice from an old man, but if you wanted one final piece I've accrued on women, here it is… don't live to regret the things you never said.'

'Do you?'

'Have regrets?'

'Yeah.'

'One or two… one or two. And the time's long passed change them.'

And whether it was his intention or not, all I can think about now is Nina.

And how royally I fucked things up.

Why did I say those things?

Why did I let it ruin the best day of my life?!

You're gonna lose that girl unless you go find her and apologise…

'When's your flight?'

'Nine-ish.'

'So, you got about seven hours to make things right?'

'How do you know I—'

'—Parents know.'

Time check — 12.22.

'Dad, I gotta go...'

'I know.'

It's not the time to hug it out.

We're not there yet. Still too much to be said.

But I'm glad we are at the hand on the shoulder stage.

'Here, take this. It's not much, but it's all I've got

on me. In case you need a jacket over there.'

'You just carry around $700 regularly?'

'I never know who I might run into.'

'Well, thanks, I appreciate it. Catch you around, old man.'

'Hope so mate. Look after yourself.'

'TAXI!'

Damn… OK then, I guess I'm running across town to her hotel.

OK, what am I going to say?

What *can* I say?

I fucked it up pretty spectacularly.

Do I wing it? Hope she opens the door and ad lib an apology?

Yeah, you know you're not great with winging it.

So what do I say?

Got any suggestions, Mr Moonlight?

No?

Maybe lead with the fact that I'm a loser? That the things we said today were just in the heat of the moment and I don't mean any of them?

No Grant… you know what you have to do.

Think I'll cut through Hyde Park, past the ANZAC memorial, it'll be quicker.

I'm so so sorry Nina.

I'm an arsehole, and you don't deserve what I said…

…It's a start.

But is it enough?

Well, despite everything, I've had a great day.

It's not the end I wanted… but when is it ever.

When I get home, I think I need a break.

From love.

From touring.

Feel what it's like being happy to spend the rest of my life with myself first before settling with someone again.

Get a dog.

I want a dog.

A marbly black French Bulldog.

Called Rocco.

'Hey Bulldog, come here. Come to mama, Rocco.'

Yep, when I get back, it's time to lay some roots and start something akin to life.

I've seen all I want of the world.

For now anyway.

This really is a great city though. I know I've only seen a hint of it, but it's got great character.

People are friendly, it's clean, safe.

But I miss home.

And it's time to return.

Speaking of which, me thinks it's time for another one of those lovely painkillers.

They've definitely taken the edge off tonight. Thank you which ever god up there is in charge of pharmies.

Well, I've soaked in enough of this ANZAC Memorial, so probably time to call this little lady a night.

'TAXI!'

KNOCK KNOCK KNOCK
'Nina? Are you in there? Nina?'

'I'm... sorry.'
KNOCK KNOCK.

KNOCK.

OK, plan B...

'Excuse me, concierge?'
  'Yes sir.'
  'Could you spare a couple of pieces of paper, so I can write a note?'
  'Certainly.'
  'Could I borrow that pen too?'
  'Of course.'
  'Thank you.'

OK brain, you don't like me and I don't particularly like you, but let's put aside our differences for tonight only and help each other out. Then I promise we can get back to despising each other tomorrow, OK?

Now... what words did she use to start this with...

"She walked into his life like..."

No...
'"Strolled, she strolled into his life."
That's it...
"She strolled into his life like... Like..."
Come on you stupid useless pink grey blob.
Work with me!!

KNOCK KNOCK KNOCK
'Nina? Are you back?'

I guess she's not here.
All I can do is slide it under her door and hope
for the best.

And now, I go to wait.

'And here's your guitar, Miss Taylor.'
'Thank you so much.'
'Will there be anything else tonight?'
'No, thank you for helping me bring this up.'
'With pleasure. Good evening.'
'Goodnight.'
And... I'm done.
I made it.
You survived one of the rottenest days of the last
year.
Have a bath, relax, then sleep it off.
Uhhh, my feet are killing me. Away with you,

shoes.

Hold up, what's that by the door?

A note…

… what's all this about then?

"She strolled into his life like a velvet freight train. This girl didn't pay much heed to subtly; a by-product of her ability to live for the now, to hell with what's lost and gone. It was a quality that would make her often misunderstood, but never easy to forget. She was truly unaware of just how beautiful she was, which served her well, by illuminating her natural grace but not letting it overshadow her other abundant qualities. But beautiful she was.

"Her lips were full, pouty. The sort that lipstick would only spoil. They were the type you'd want to spend a whole weekend in bed with, forcing you to call in sick on Monday in the hope of chasing that one last ephemeral kiss. Even still, there was something misplaced in her broken smile; something that said more than her words could articulate, about the pain she was protecting, and always would. But even beaming through a half bitten lower lip, it put all around her to shame.

"If only he paid closer attention to her eyes now — were they turquoise? Aqua? Sea-green? A triviality he'd concluded, as they held a warmth and understanding that he'd long thought improbable to find in a girl.

"A girl? A woman? Neither term seemed quite right for her. She fit somewhere neatly in-between, inhabiting the better qualities of both. And with her mellifluous tones, she had the ability to put him at ease with an unaccountable velocity, and he felt more able to be himself in her presence than with any woman, or man, hitherto. Or possibly ever again.

"So, in spite of all the danger that velvet train brought him, giving him the 'best' worst day of his life, he'd gladly wait on that platform until his last moment, hoping for a glimpse of the promise that that day held, forever regretting that he never thanked her. Because, Beatles fan or not, she was truly someone for whom risking heartbreak would always be worth the gamble."

...I knew you had it in you, Local.

And what's he drawn here on the back?

A map.

"If I haven't completely screwed up, I'd love to see you one last time. I'll be waiting at this location, my favourite night spot by the harbour, and if you come, you'll find me sitting high in the second last tree, where I'll be waiting all night, G x."

12.59...

Is this really the hour for a respectable young lady to be traipsing all over a foreign city?

...probably not.

The question is though, am I a respectable young lady...?

CHAPTER TWENTY-ONE
ONE AM

This is crazy.

It's stupid.

She's not gonna come.

As if she would come.

I'm an idiot.

She's a huge star. And I blew it by insulting her.

But now I've trapped myself here all night.

Stuck fourteen feet off the ground on the branch of this stupid Morton Bay fig.

I should leave.

But I can't. Just in case on the 0.0000037% chance she does come, well… I can't not be here for that, can I?

So, I definitely can't leave in case she does come by.

Which she won't…

…Maybe I can wait a little bit longer then, write a note.

No, not another note.

I think if she did come — not gonna happen — but if she did, and I wasn't here, that would be "note" enough.

So I can't leave.

As pointless as this is, I'm stuck here.

All.

Damned.

Night.

'Hey Local.'

She came!!!

'Hey.'

'So did you know there's a breed of deer that can jump higher than the average house?'

'Ahhh, no, I did not know that.'

'Yeah, it's true. A breed found primarily in the middle of Canada. They say it's because these deer have especially strong hind legs. Well that, plus houses can't jump.'

'I've never been happier to hear a terrible joke in my life.'

'Interesting location you picked. You couldn't have just waited outside the hotel?'

'Where's the romance in that?'

'Oh I forgot, you're the hopeless romantic type.'

'You've pigeon-holed me.'

'So... I got your note. Obviously.'

'Oh, yeah, that. Sorry it was rushed—'

'—It was beautiful. I suspected you had it within you, without your pride stopping you from writing it.'

'I'm glad you liked it.'

'I did. So... you gonna invite me up or are we just gonna be shouting at each other from different latitudes all night?'

'Of course. You need a hand getting up.'

'I'm good... Almost there.'

'Watch that branch.'

'It's fine… And… there we go.'

'There we do go.'

'And here we both are.'

'Here we both are indeed.'

'Wow. I can see why it's your favourite spot. This view is amazing.'

'It is pretty spectacular. I've been saying this a lot lately — quite liberally today if I'm honest — but I'm really sorry for how I behaved, after the show.'

'I know.'

'It was not called for, I completely overreacted. I regret it all. I'm really sorry.'

'Apology accepted. I'm sorry if today was painful.'

'I was being a shit. For a day that shouldn't have been, it turned out OK… better than OK. Kinda very great really… And I've been thinking about what you said. And it's what most people I know have been too gutless to say to me — or maybe they have, and I haven't been listening…. I fucked everything up so badly, treating my friend's like garbage, pushing them away, taking them for granted, that one by one, they drifted away.'

'You're not the first or the last to find a friend in the drink after a break-up.'

'I know. But what you said made me think about it all — about "anywhere I go, there I am". It's true. I'm gonna be just as miserable anywhere until I realise that I'm in control of it all. You know, I was thinking back over what we've talked about today and I realised I've just been holding on with anger to a girl who was never gonna make me happy, cause I gave up chasing what made me happy.'

Her warm smile says more than words.

This is comfortable silence.

Which I break.

'Can I ask you a question?'

'Shoot Local.'

'Do you shake up the life of a stranger in every city you breeze through?'

'Every single one.'

'Thought so.'

And then, it finally happens.

In the silence, her eyes lock on mine, longer than a friendly conversation allows.

And our faces inch monumentally slowly closer.

And then…

…we kiss.

Gently at first, just pressing our lips together.

Then she licks my lower lip.

And I wrap my tongue around hers.

Before we know it, Sydney dissipates…

…And the only thing in our singular world is each other.

'Hey Local, do you think twelve hours is too soon for a rebound?'

CHAPTER TWENTY-TWO

TWO AM

'So, this is your room huh?

'Yep.'

'This is the rock star life?'

'So they tell me.'

'I was expecting a few more manservants.'

'Gave 'em the night off. Do you want a drink?'

'Ummm… What are you having?'

'Vodka. Want one?'

'Actually, no. I think I'm OK.'

'That's good cause I actually think I gave you all the alcohol from the mini bar this morning and they haven't restocked it.'

'That's luck for you.'

God…. Why am I feeling so nervous?!?

Why are you acting all weird Ryder?

Act naturally.

WHAT IS WRONG WITH YOU!!!

You're in her room, this is good.

I want you Nina.

This is what you want. Isn't it?!

I guess I can't look past the fact that she's infinitely cool and incredible and I'm just some twat who writes hostel reviews.

Stop it! Don't put her on a pedestal and ruin this, you nonce!

'You OK?'

'Yeah. Yeah. Sorry, was just checking out the… carpet.'

'As you do.'

'So, ummm… when's your flight?'

'Ten maybe, or eleven.'

'Hmmm. Melbourne's nice. Nicer than Sydney.'

'I doubt that.'

'Umm yeah.'

What are you doing you dummy?

You're making this really weird.

Stopping thinking and just go with it.

OK, so she's kissing you now.

OK.

It's fine.

Her hands are roaming now.

Down your back.

Under your belt.

Into your pants.

Don't think about performance anxiety.

Don't think about performance anxiety.

Don't think about…

…you've thought about it—

'—You know, ahhh, we don't have to… you know… like if you wanted to keep the day… like, special or whatever. We don't have to do… this. Or whatever.'

'Oh.'

'You know I don't want you thinking I was like

just, you know, in it to do this… I didn't plan, I wasn't just trying you know to, ummm… you know.'

SHUT THE FUCK UP YOU FUCKING IDIOT!

I fucking hate you brain.

'No, it's OK. That's fine, we can just, hang.'

Why!!!!

Why did you have to spontaneously put a floppy cock into my head NOW!!!!

'So…'

'…So.'

'So, what do you think you would be doing right now, right this second, if you'd never crossed paths with me at the airport?'

'Wow, well, if I'd never met you, I'd, let's see it's 2.19 so, I think I'd be in Amsterdam right now. But… on any other given night, I'd probably be sitting at some café, skimming through my book for the hundredth time, thoroughly bored, counting down the seconds for something more exciting to do.'

'Well, let's do that then.'

'Oh, OK.'

'Do you know a good all night café around here?'

'Yeah, there's a place not far.'

'Let's go.'

Congratulations Grant, once again royally fucking up a completely amazing situation.

But let's go drink coffee.

You

God

Damn

Mother
Flipping
F-WIT!!

'Two long blacks thanks.'

'Anything else guys? The wild honey pie is freshly baked and frankly, pretty amazing.'

'I'm OK, do you want any?'

'No, not right now thanks.'

'OK, two long blacks, you got it.'

'This place is cute. Cozy. I can see how you'd be drawn to it, especially on a winter's night.'

'It's got its charm. You definitely see some characters pass through here.'

'Ahh, my kind of people.'

This is SOOOO MUCH better than being back in her room.

You fucktard.

'So… Oh, I just wanted to say that you were amazing tonight.'

'Thanks.'

'At your show, I mean. You were amazing at your show.'

'I know. Oh, they have a jukebox.'

'Yep, it's pretty great. Full of original 45's from the 50's and 60's.'

'Oh, we gotta put something on then.'

'Here's a couple bucks.'

'Come choose with me.'

'OK.'

'Three for two dollars, bargain! OK, we pick one each and then we'll close our eyes and randomly select the third.'

'Done.'

'Oooooooh ooh ohh, Carl Perkins' original "Blue Suede Shoes", that's me. Your turn.'

'Sooooo much pressure, picking songs with a professional musician, I gotta make a solid pick here… give me a moment, don't want to waste it…'

'Take your time. No rush… So, you really have no musical ability at all?'

'I've got a singing voice that makes the deaf thankful for their predicament and absolutely zip musical co-ordination whatsoever. Two left hands, full of thumbs.'

'Show me. Your hands.'

I love the way her fingers gently touch mine.

It's making the hairs stand up on the back of my neck.

Which I guess is almost as good as sex.

Not.

'You have such dainty — can I say that word, dainty — hands.'

'You can say it Local, I have midget's hands.'

'I wouldn't say that. Do you find that hard playing guitar?'

'A little initially — a few bar chords that are near impossible to play, but you know, you make use of what you have.'

'Oh, I think I've found my song.'

'What?'

'"Ain't No Way".'

'Aretha! Great choice Local. Gimme five.'

207

'OK, so now we close our eyes and blindly pick the last one?'

'And ready... Press those buttons and... what have we got?'

'Ha, "Lucy In The Sky With Diamonds".'

'Nice... Oh, our coffees are there.'

'Thank you kind sir. But getting back to that conversation, if you *did* have musical skills — say I had a magic wand and could grant Grant unprecedented musical stupendousness — would you want to be a solo performer or would you be in a band?'

'Oh, definitely a band. Despite the absent musical prowess, I used to spend hours late at night having conversations with mates — who were equally musically challenged — trying to come up with what we call our band.'

'And what did you settle on?'

'Well, we decided we were gonna start out as a garage rock band and go huge as "The Mystery Bruises". But then we'd go through a big band break up — you know, drummer OD's on coke on the toilet eating a kebab and everyone ending up in rehab, but then we all clean up and reform as "The Tender Fucks". Then we'd all get old disgracefully and do fifteen farewell tours and then finally die when a drunk roadie drives the tour bus over a cliff and we all go out in a huge ball of flames.'

'Sounds like you've put some thought into this masterplan.'

'You got to have something to fall back on, you know, for safety.'

'Indeed.'

'It's just smart.'

'So... I gotta say Local, that was impressive back there, in the hotel room.'

'Oh?'

'I've never seen defeat snatched from the jaws of victory so effectively. You could teach courses in it.'

'I... yeah, I'm sorry. I was stupid. I let my mind over think things.... I haven't been with anyone for a long time and I was just worried... thinking too much about fucking it up, that I self-prophesied the fuck up...'

'You finished your coffee?'

'Yeah.'

'Then shut the fuck up, pay the bill and take me back to my room.'

I don't need to be told twice.

OK, that's a lie, but *this* time, I don't, and I'm leading her by the hand, out the door and back to her room, before Aretha has a chance to hit the bridge.

CHAPTER TWENTY-THREE

THREE AM

I have to take charge with him, that's just how it is.

It's not the first time I've had to, but... it's been a while since I have.

It's kinda sweet, his complete and utter awkwardness.

But I'm not complaining... because this feels real.

This feels like something I want to remember.

I want to remember this. Memory, don't pass me by, OK?

I want to remember his hand firm on the back of my neck.

His fingers pulsing as he holds me to his lips.

I want to remember the way his tongue pushes against mine, not too hard, just right.

I want to remember the small circular motions he works it in.

I want to remember his hand sliding up my left thigh, the back of his hand rubbing against my silk underwear, almost wet through, with anticipation that it's finally happening.

That this is really happening.

I want to remember how he manages to fumble and look nervously apologetic as he fails to unhook my bra.

I want to remember the curve of his top lip as he asks me to help him unlatch it.

I want to remember the kisses, so soft, down my left side… from my armpit… to my hip that make me squirm with ticklish delight… hmmmm.

I want to remember his low, breathy moans as his kisses get more intense, and his sweat starting to bead from his pores.

And how it feels as his sweat mixes with mine.

But… his tongue starting to get more exploratory in my mouth, until I tell him to go slower, *that* I can forget…

Though I never want to forget him fingering me, his fingertips getting wetter as I rhythmically pulse against them.

How he licks each nipple, then gently blows warm air across them.

And how him doing that made me break out in goosebumps.

Or the rough sensation of his chewed nails as he drags his fingers across my ass.

How his cock feels as it pushes into me.

The gasp of anticipation as it entered.

Deeper.

And that half smile as he looks at me, from above.

I want to remember the averageness of his body, not toned, not overweight, just average. Inoffensive. Normal.

I want to remember his smell, his rough smell.

The seawater, the sweat... the engine grease, the coffee and, ha, just a hint of sweet and sour barbecued pork.

I want to remember it all.

I need to remember this all.

CHAPTER TWENTY-FOUR

FOUR AM

'Soooo… how about that silence huh?'

'Local, be quiet and enjoy the moment. And give me a cigarette.'

'You can't do that in here.'

'Watch me. Lighter?'

Where is it…? Damn, I think I left it at dad's.

'I don't think have one.'

'I might, pass me my bag. Thanks, ah-ha, there we go.'

'A box of Redheads, huh, Quintessentially Australian. And there you go, breaking yet another law. What's that take the tally up to now?'

'Gotta be in the triple digits at least.'

'Go on, pass it here then, give me a drag.'

Ahhhh…

…this breaking the law stuff is fun.

'That was pretty amazing, before.'

'Hmmmm, yeah, yeah it was. You seem to know what you're doing Local.'

Really?!

I mean—

'—Thanks. You're quite the expert yourself.'

What was that?!

Dumb is what it was.

Stop the pillow talk nitwit, you're rubbish at it.

'Hand me the matchbox again.'

'Here you go… and, you've emptied its contents all over the duvet because?'

'Count 'em'?

'What?'

'How many matches are there?'

'I dunno. Like thirty?

'No, count them exactly.'

'Fine, one, two, three…'

I love the way her slender, pale fingers pick up each individual match then carefully places them back in their hold… while her lips silently count out each one.

'Forty two.'

'OK, so forty two times.'

'Forty two times what?'

'The next forty two times you light a cigarette, you'll think of tonight. And me. Let's think of it as a kind of insurance policy.'

'Cute. But I promise you, I won't need a box of matches to forget tonight any time soon.'

There's that smile.

If only I could bottle that smile and keep it with me forever.

'Are you ashing in the vase?'

'Yeah, there's no ashtray.'

'Could be that because, as the "NO SMOKING" signs subtly allude to, that there's no smoking in this room?'

'Could be.'

'You know there's a TV over there too if you wanted to throw it out the window and really be a rock star.'

'I can think of something a little less anarchic but way more fun than that.'

'Oh yeah?'

'Yeah. Grab your clothes, we're going on an adventure.'

CHAPTER TWENTY-FIVE
FIVE AM

Well, as I walked up the aisle onto the plane departing Tokyo last night, the last thing I thought I would be doing a day later would be watching the sunrise on a beach.

I did not think I would be watching the sunrise on a beach having not slept.

I did not think I would be watching the sunrise on a beach having not slept, wet and naked.

I did not think I would be watching the sunrise on a beach having not slept, wet and naked with someone — if the circumstance were... different — I could fall for.

'So, it's tomorrow.'

'The day they say never knows.'

'And never comes.'

'I wish for once they were right.'

'But it's brought you the start of a new life, right Local?'

'That it has. Thing is though... do I want it?'

'When's your flight?'

'Three hours... I wonder what we missed in the world while we let it slip by yesterday.'
'Probably nothing important.'
'Yeah... Yeah, I think you're mostly likely right.'
And now I'm crazily thinking of postponing my flight, staying in Sydney for a bit longer.
Or travelling to Amsterdam.
Something...
Anything to spend a bit more time with him.
But is that practical?
No, of course it isn't...
Is it possible?

...Anything is.

Question is... should I do it?
Should I cancel the show in Melbourne tonight, or push it back?
Should I ask him to come to Melbourne?
I could pay him, as my entourage.
God, how tacky did that sound?
What is this I'm feeling right now?
Is this lust?
Love?
It can't be. It doesn't work that way.
Not in the way that I believe it to work.

...All I know is I don't want this to end right now.

But... how else can it end, other than here on a beach at sunrise?

What realistic outcome can happen from this?

'Here comes the sun.'

'Little darling.'

'You know the worst thing about Sydney's beaches.'

'Something you left off that extensive list Local?'

'Ha. The sun doesn't set over the water.'

'Well… it's gotta rise somewhere.'

Please something, anything, happen to keep this going a bit longer.

Please?

'Are you thinking what I'm thinking?'

'I don't know Local? What are you thinking?'

'I was thinking how did we manage to do so much in just one day?'

…No Local, I was not thinking what you were thinking…

…not at all.

CHAPTER TWENTY-SIX

SIX AM

There's something really revolting about the way clothes cling to your wet body.

They'll dry soon enough I guess.

'You can already feel it's gonna be another scorcher today.'

'Hmmm…'

'How's your coffee?'

'Good. Yours?'

'Good.'

'Good.'

Is this where we've run out of things to say? On the slow walk back to her hotel, with both of us knowing this is the end.

If only I knew how she felt.

If only there was a sign this meant anything to her.

I want to believe it did.

But, this is the life she leads. Probably happens

to her all the time… why should I think I've made any more of an impression on her than anyone else?

Her life is fleeting moments of interactions with people she'll never cross paths with again.

It's almost too hopeless to bring up the possibility of more time together, it would be comical to even suggest "hey Nina, I wanna be your man, whatcha say?".

Just clock it up to yet another unrequited love in your life.

But why does it feel so much more than that?

'So…'

'So… here we are, back at your hotel.'

'Yep, here it is.'

Why can't I make eye contact with her?

Why can't I tell what she's feeling?

'Look, this is stupid. Let's just shake hands, say goodbye, make it quick and be on our ways.'

'Just like ripping off a band aid, huh?'

'Exactly Local… exactly.'

And she's holding her hand out.

Which I guess that means I have to put mine out too.

The thing is I want to grab her and hold her and if not *not* let go of her ever… at least not let go of her until what we've had between us no longer feel so tangible.

'Don't leave me hanging Local.'

And so reluctantly, I shake her hand, like I

know I have to…

Cause it's the only way this can end…

'You know what? Fuck you.'

'Sorry?'

'You and that fucking bottle of vodka. Why couldn't you have just grabbed a coffee? Or have turned up to some other café this morning? Then we could have just passed each other by and never known the difference. But, you come along and I end up having pretty much the greatest day I've ever had with anybody, anywhere, ever.'

'You know what's funny, I did go into another cafe this morning.'

'Really?'

'Yeah, there weren't any cute guys in there.'

'See, all the puzzle pieces, for whatever reason, had come together to make today happen. So, fuck you. Fuck you for being you. And fuck you for being English. And fuck airline policies. And fuck fucking vodka. And fuck fucking Sydney. And fuck your awful jokes. Especially fuck your awful jokes. And fuck today.'

'Fuck 'em all, right?'

'Yeah… fuck 'em all.'

Then, I see her bottom lip start to shake, ever so slightly and it's only when she pulls her hand away that I realise that I've been holding it that whole time.

And she shouts—

'TAXI!'

And as its brakes squeal pulling up… I know this is the end.

'You getting in love?'

'He is. He's going to the airport.'

I've never seen sadder eyes move slower, as she looks from me to the taxi, which she's willing me into.

'I... I want to stay here. With you.'

'But... I'm flying to Melbourne in a few hours. And you're moving to Amsterdam.'

'I'll cancel my ticket.'

If *don't be stupid* had a visual cue, the look she just gave me would pretty much encapsulate it.

'But... I don't want to go, I want to spend more time with you.'

'...Goodbye has to come at some point, Local.'

And in spite of that logic, I want to find the words to argue against it.

To say of course we can make it work.

'Does it though?'

Her hand feels warm on my cheek.

'Everyone needs a one that got away.'

And I know that we've come to the end.

And the blaring horn from the taxi breaks the silence and pulls us back to reality, as any words I was trying to find to change this situation, tumble into the space between today and forever.

'Go.'

And like that, it ends.

I look back one last time, hoping the words fall from her lips, to tell me to stay...

...But they don't.

I don't know if this passenger car door is incredibly heavy...

...or my arms just have no desire to close it.

'Domestic or international mate?'

'International.'

And like the flame on a candle that's burned out, she gets smaller and smaller in the rear window as we drive off to whatever life awaits me.

And like that, he's gone.

What just happened?

Gone in the blink of an eye... hello, goodbye, that's it.

Why did he... I mean, how did he come to mean so much so quickly?

It was just a day.

Twenty four hours, that's it.

Love doesn't form that soon.

It can't.

I know it can't.

So why do I feel like I've lost something I'll never get back?

And why didn't I kiss him?!

Why on Earth did I just say shaking hands was the best thing to do?!

You nitwit!

Why didn't I grab him and hold him close and kiss him?

WHY? WHY? WHY?—

'—NINA!'

Just like that, he's running back up the street towards me, with a very irate taxi driver screaming at him.

And then, he's back in front of me.

Breathless.

'I'm not leaving with just a handshake.'

Then he's kissing me.

And it's incredible.

Like the kind of kiss people write songs about.

…I don't want this to end.

Fuck, he's a great kisser.

…would be even more perfect I'm sure when he brushes his teeth though.

'Bye Nina.'

'Later Local.'

And he walks back to the taxi and into the ether.

At least, we ended with a kiss.

'OOOOH, HEY LOCAL, WAIT!!'

'What is it?'

'You forgot this.'

And I return his friends, salvaged at the airport, back safely in his hands.

'You've been carrying this the whole time?'

'Waiting for the right moment to give it back, you know.'

A final kiss.

And there's that smile.

That cheeky, gorgeous smile.

I'll find you again one day smile.

Even if I have to travel across the universe, I will find you again.

'I'm sorry for jumping out the cab mate.'
    'Don't bloody do it again or I'll chuck you out.'
    'I'm sorry... had to be done.'
    It did have to be done.
    How could I leave without a kiss?
    And what a kiss though.
    She's such a great kisser.
    Those lips of hers.
    Uhhh.

Oh shit, I haven't brushed my teeth since yesterday morning.

    ...I hope she didn't notice.

OK... how much time do I have until my flight?
    Two-ish hours.
    I'm so tired... hopefully I'll have a kip on the plane.
    Think I'll pack up quickly, jump in the shower and grab some breakfast at the airport.
    OK, shoes, in the case...
    Stinky black dress, you can go in the laundry bag with the undies.
    ...Mmm oh, my computer, and where's the

charger?

How did it get under the bed?

Guitar... And the new set of spare strings, in the front pocket.

Can't forget the newly acquired street sign from Penny Lane in Bondi, you can go in the guitar case too for safe keeping.

Anything else?

Ahh yes, "The Lonely Planet Guide to Sydney".

Hmmm, I usually bin these once I've left a city. But I might make an exception and hold onto this one.

Let's have a quick squiz... so I saw the Opera House, The Rocks, check... Bondi... lovely Manly... Camp Cove. So many wonderful places, and you're all far more beautiful than these words can describe.

And what's this?

Something he's written on the back page.

"You still owe me $20!"

Ha! You cheeky git.

Time check — 6.37.

Well, Sydney, I guess this is really it, this time.

Thank you for giving me one last glimpse of what you had hidden up your sleeve.

...I'm sorry I doubted you.

Goodbye, you magnificent bastard.

Don't forget to write.

I can't believe she held onto this book.

I thought it was lost for good.

But I tell you one thing Franny & your little mate Zooey, you're far too valuable now to ever leave my side again.

Oh, what's just fallen out of it?

A ten dollar note?

Ha! She must have slipped it inside.

And scrawled a little note inside the cover,

"Come and find me, you get the rest x"

A challenge Miss Taylor?

"Come and find me, you get the rest x"

In that case Mystery Guitar Girl, your challenge is accepted.

Your challenge is most definitely accepted.

…she liked me.

She really liked *me*.

And I… love her.

I'm going to find her.

If I have to look here, there and everywhere…

… I will.

Thank you so much for reading. If you enjoyed this book, please leave a review on Amazon or Goodreads (or both if you're feeling generous) to help other readers find it.

Reviews really help independent writers get seen by the widest audience.

For exclusive content and to stay informed about the upcoming feature film release of "Any Girl Who Loves The Beatles…" please sign up to my mailing list at www.nickpollack.com/author and if you want to get in touch with me, drop me a note at nick@nickpollackauthor.com

My sincerest thanks and appreciation for helping bring this project to life go to Ryan Hayward, Aaron Bush, Damon Lane, Diane Drake, Emily Anderton, Beatrice Neumann, Stephanie Higgins, Simon Harding, Alex & Tamsin, Jacqui Louez Schoorl, Louis Schoorl, Jeremy Shabo, Anna Samson, Leigh Pickford, Tom Carney, Andy Abraham, Lyn Cottier, Phil Middleton, John Hilary Shepherd, Marcus Gillezeau, Sally Caplan, Simon Crowe, Russell Webber, Joan Sauers, Nicole Dade, Screen Australia, Screen NSW, Sydney Festival, the City of Sydney, Adrian & Matt and mum & dad.

21938848R00138

Printed in Great Britain
by Amazon